Claiming Trinity

Wiccan Haus Book 14

By
Kali Willows

Copyright © 2016 by Kali Willows
ISBN: 978-1-68361-021-2
Cover art by Fiona Jayde

Published by Decadent Publishing Company, LLC
Look for us online at:
www.decadentpublishing.com

~A Note from the Author~

Thank you for choosing Claiming Trinity for your reading pleasure! Trinity has a compelling story, about a woman trying to overcome elements beyond her control. Her life takes a turn for the worst and she accepts an impromptu invitation to a fantastic island dedicated to healing practices for the guests, both para and human alike. It's filled with suspense and steamy intrigue as she delves into sacred realms to seek out the truth behind attacks on her, while the temptation of not one, but two smoldering, sexy men sweep her off her feet. Will she survive the life and death circumstances? Or perhaps find romance among the ruins of her career and personal life?

Happy Reading,

Kali Willows

Dedication

To my readers, and FAN-ADDICTS, without you, my stories would end when the final words are typed. With you, they live on forever.

To Dominique Eastwick, thank you for welcoming me the Wiccan Haus world, a place I never want to leave.

Welcome to the Wiccan Haus

Something Wiccan this way comes to a mystical mysterious island where authors get to play and bring their love stories to life. At the Wiccan Haus you will meet Rekkus, Cyrus, Sage, Sarka, Cemil, and Myron, all of whom return in most if not all the stories. Yes each one will eventually get their HEA as well.

We hope you enjoy the stories from all the authors and return time and again to keep up with the staff and meet new characters along the way. But fear not if this is your first or twenty-first story each book stands on its own.

Prologue

T he gruesome scenes had stained Trinity's memory for an eternity. Most days, she maintained a professional ability to shut off her emotions and recall when in session. Until these past few weeks, she had never lost control over her skill to push the images out of her head when needed. In fact, the pressure against her temples right this second threatened to explode her head into a thousand pieces.

"Trinity?" His gentle voice snagged her attention.

Her breath caught in her throat. "Excuse me." She worked to shove the painful visions of mortality from her mind. Trinity gathered the papers in front of her, tidied the pile, and tucked her fountain pen into the holder on the desktop.

"It would seem our grief therapist is in need of a little respite herself, Sage?" Cemil reached across the mahogany desk and patted Trinity's hand. "It's a good thing this is our last visit." His long blond hair cascaded around his broad shoulders, and his icy-blue eyes sparkled.

"I agree. I have just the item she needs...." The flaxen beauty at his side, whose eyes matched the same stunning color as her counterpart, opened her large canvas bag and fished through it. "Ah, this should help." She tugged out a small blue organza satchel with tied drawstrings and handed it to Trinity.

"What's this?" She accepted the filled bag and breathed in the tranquil floral scent.

"It's a pouch of lavender, a few other herbal ingredients, and some rose quartz, onyx, and moonstones." Sage gathered her canvas bag and stood.

"For...?"

"Keep it under your pillow at night. It will help you sleep better. And keep it with you through the day...it will balance your energy."

"I didn't say anything about not sleeping," she protested, her cheeks warming. "This is your therapy session, not mine. I can't accept this." She gestured to give it back.

Sage waved it away.

Trinity tried to hand it to Cemil. "No thanks. I sleep fine, but then again, I'm not swarmed with visions of death and massacre."

"I-I...." Stunned at his accuracy, she swallowed hard. "I'm familiar with your talents and admire them, really I do. But I'm not seeking counsel right now."

"Oh, but you need to." Sage grinned.

Cemil cleared his throat, rose from his seat, and stood at his sister's side. "Trinity, thank you so much. I know Sarka and Cyrus weren't very receptive to your assistance—they never came to see you at all, in fact—but we appreciate all you've done to help us work through this"—his chin quivered—"everything."

"It's my pleasure. Please accept my sincere apologies. My awareness is a little off today." *Today?* She downright lied. Her attention had been off for weeks. She stood to see them out.

Sage paused and faced her. "Trinity, you know who we are and what we do."

In their monthly meetings together since the siblings came to see her a year ago, she had grown to find Sage characteristically soft and flaky in the way she talked. Her current demeanor of narrowed eyes and lack of cheerful smile came across as firmer than usual.

"The Syndicate has tried to make amends. The island is a huge success. We discussed it with Sarka and Cyrus, and we would all be pleased if you would join us as our guest for a week."

Trinity's throat grew thick. "You all discussed me?" Unsure if she should be offended or honored, she wrapped her arms around herself.

"You've helped us through the most impossible circumstances, and we are better prepared to help others now. We want to extend the same gift to you." Sage shifted her focus to the contents of her bulky bag. "Caregivers burn out, too."

"After all you've been through yourself in the past six months," Cemil continued, as though they had prepared to tag-team this speech beforehand, "it's no wonder you can't shut your talents off anymore."

She gasped. "I never said—"

"We are paras, you are a para. We understand, the way you did with us. The flashbacks, the trauma, the loss. Even psychologists need a little therapy with life's tragedies. There's no shame in it," he affirmed. "It took us years to ask for help. Please don't wait as long as we did."

She exhaled an exhausted breath. To have the same words of wisdom she'd offered the resistant siblings used against her proved unfair at best. "Thank you. I know you're right," she conceded.

In fact, their profound losses occurred more than six years prior, but they'd needed time before they were able to seek out her professional assistance.

"Ah ha!" Sage blurted out. She yanked an oblong black leather case from her bag and presented it to Trinity.

"Another gift? I can't accept this, really." She shook her head.

"They were custom made." Sage tucked the box into her hand. "Sarka had her friend here in the city make them for you. It's a tool, not a gift."

Trinity lifted the case and opened it. Inside was a spectacular set of pewter-frame glasses, with engraved Celtic knotwork around the edge and rose-colored lenses. She glanced up in awe. "They're unique and gorgeous."

"They're enchanted, designed to give your senses a little bit of a break." Cemil grinned. He picked them up and extended the intricate arms then inched them over her ears and settled them on her nose. "Can you see our auras now?"

"You know I can see auras?" Her chest tightened. In all their time together, they'd never once discussed her abilities. But then again, they talked about theirs in great detail. She shouldn't be surprised at how much they knew about her.

"Of course we do." Sage giggled. "These dull your acute perceptions of auras, since your system is on overload. It affects your sleep and every waking interaction with humans and para alike. To live and work in New York City would strain anyone, but a para who practices psychology? Talk about burnout waiting to happen."

"Given your recent loss and the whole situation with your parents, we feel, if you agree to join us, we can help you find some balance and peace in exchange for the very gifts you've bestowed upon us. It would be an honor if you let us pamper you for a week." Cemil flashed a playful pout.

"I can't, I've got my patients, and...." she lied.

Her business had dwindled over the months. The mundane were not in need of her unstable sessions. Who in their right mind, or otherwise, wanted to experience their therapist suffer from horrific flashbacks of post-traumatic stress disorder in the middle of their therapy? And when she picked up on their traumas in a visual play-by-play, it wiped out every ounce of resiliency she had left. Eight patients had cancelled in recent weeks. Sage and Cemil were her last two, and, after today, they were done. In essence, she had no practice left.

The sibs knew what they were talking about. Only six months ago, she'd foreseen her uncle's brutal murder and been powerless to stop it. Her precognitive tears of blood had confirmed his death would be inevitable, just like with both her parents.

"You'll need this, too." Sage handed her a small object.

"What is it?" She examined the triangular, swirling symbol.

"It's a triple spiral labyrinth." Sage ran her finger over the carved detail. "It reminds me of you, beautiful, complicated, and unique, all in one." She stepped back and the corners of her mouth retreated with a mischievous grin. "Everyone gets their exclusive charm to enter the portal."

"Portal?"

"Yes, it's how paras arrive to the island. Humans take the ferry. Portal transportation takes place at sunset at Portal Central in the para capital city. You can't get on or off the island without this. It's your boarding pass, so to speak." Cemil folded her fingers over the trinket.

"I haven't agreed." She shook her head, tears blurring her eyes.

"The arrangements have all been made. We will see you next Saturday." Sage handed her an envelope. "We sensed urgency for you to attend, so there will be no delay. Details are in there. We have two portal sites. Given your situation, we've all agreed it's best to have you arrive directly at the Wiccan Haus where there will be less traffic and stimulation for you to contend with."

Chapter One

With a deep breath and her Wiccan Haus charm in hand, Trinity folded her completed checklist of items to pack and shoved it into her pocket. She clutched the handle of her suitcase and mustered the courage to step into the portal.

In a flash, lights swirled around her, the sensation of gravity dissipated, her body lightened, and her limbs lingered in the air. She floated up, twisted, and spun on the spot. A faint but deep voice echoed in the distance. "Incoming."

In the blink of an eye, she bounced through the end of the portal, crashing into three large, burly men and toppling over a dark-haired stranger.

"Whoa!" He stopped their rolling together and landed on his back. Warm hands gripped her as she came to rest on top of his rock-solid chest, face to face. He chuckled. "You okay, princess?"

The sweetness of his warm breath brushed her lips and tingles of electricity ran over her sides where his hands held her steady. A delectable aroma of amber and patchouli wafted past her nose. Trinity leaned closer to his neck and inhaled then jerked back, lost in the depths of his dark eyes and chiseled features.

His stare penetrated her and his touch stirred something deep inside. "I'm...oh, my...." She bit her lip.

"Are you hurt?" He frowned.

"No." She rested her palms on his chest. *But I don't think I would notice if I was. My word, you're handsome.* Warmth curled around her spine, followed by giddy tickles in her tummy. Her body responded to the contact and lulled her other senses. In the next instant, she snapped out of her lustful daze. "I'm so sorry." She eased to sitting.

His hands settled on her hips. "I'm not."

Trinity's cheeks burned with embarrassment at the sudden realization she now straddled the stranger she had tackled. "By the gods, please tell me this did not just happen." She slung her leg over to kneel on the floor and scrambled up. Another set of hands gripped her under the arms and lifted her to her feet.

"You landed pretty hard, are you sure you didn't get hurt?" A second hunk straightened her glasses and brushed her shoulder off.

"I had a cushion to break my fall." She smoothed back her hair to find her tight bun had loosened. She brushed away the rogue locks, and her focus landed on another delectable vision.

Damn her glasses. The rose lenses tinted the colors she tried to see, but she would bet her life she gazed up into a brilliant set of emerald eyes, and maybe his shoulder-length hair held an auburn hue? Tall, dark, and yummy. Her kind of fantasy come true.

"If that isn't the most embarrassing entrance I've ever made, I don't know what is." She rubbed her temples and huffed with despair. Pressure pounded in her head and had worsened over the week. This situation didn't help in the least.

The first guy she knocked down had gotten to his feet. There stood a strapping, six-foot-two, rugged man—perhaps six inches taller than her—with broad shoulders and sculpted arms. His skin-tight ebony T-shirt left little to the imagination as muscles rippled beneath the flimsy material. His fitted cargo pants showcased muscular thighs. Black work boots added to the rugged appeal of this virile stranger. Streams of black ink peeked out from beneath his collar and both sleeves—possibly some serious tribal tattoos? He had the face of Adonis, shoulder-length hair as black as night, and full lips.

"Trinity." A third man approached, another unfamiliar face, with piercing amber eyes, dark hair, and dressed all in black with work boots. "I'm Rekkus, head of security."

"Oh...hello." The Rowans' description of the large tiger with an edge was bang on. "I'm sorry to crash your party," she muttered as her cheeks blazed.

Trinity glanced around the small room, horrified to discover her suitcase had tumbled, too, along with a few duffle bags. Her belongings lay strewn across the floor. She scampered to gather her clothes and stuffed them into her case. All three men helped.

"Thanks." She bit her lips and held her breath. The crash victim handed her a collection of her bras and underwear. "Guess I'll need those, too."

She shifted her gaze to the floor to avoid their penetrating stares and found she had also managed to destroy a rack of brochures. "Good grief, I'm on a roll." Trinity sulked and reached to pick up the scattered papers.

"It's okay." Rekkus gripped her wrist. "I've got this. Let's get you checked in before you take out any more of my trainees."

"Trainees?" She blinked at the men. "What are you

training for?"

"We work...in the forces...." Hunk Number Two stammered.

"We're here for extra ass-kicking by the drill sergeant-major here," the first one chimed in and waved with a smirk to Rekkus. "Hi, Trinity, my name is Arawn." He held out his powerful hand.

"It's so great to...um, bump into you." She accepted his handshake.

"The pleasure is all mine." He didn't release his grip but locked his hungry gaze on hers.

Her core rippled as she penetrated his mental shield, his lustful wishes an open book to her. It felt a little dirty to explore his thoughts without his consent, but oh how easy he made it to read him, more so than most paras she'd encountered.

Rekkus cleared his throat with a tinge of impatience. "And this is Kane."

Trinity turned to the second man who had helped her up. "Kane." She accepted his handshake as well and drank in his enchanting stare. Clothed in the same attire as the first guy, he sported a similar physique, just a tad taller and a little leaner, but every muscle as defined and chiseled as the first one. *Damn!*

He inspected her from head to toe with wide eyes. "Wow, you're gorgeous." He cleared his throat. "I mean...your glasses...gorgeous."

Butterflies pole-vaulted in her stomach with the simple touch of his hand. His continued gaze into her eyes caused the apex between her thighs to warm. *Oh, Hades, another one filled with lust?* What had she stumbled into, a sailor's shore leave? Two horny men with forward, wanton desire oozing from their pores, both easier to read than clients who sought her out and paid for her intuitive services. If only she could not know everyone else's thoughts, she might actually get to relax on this island.

"I've, uh, wow! I gotta go." She snatched up her suitcase and bolted from the room.

"Down the hall to your right. Check in with Myron," Rekkus grumbled after her.

No way could she handle any more run-ins with gorgeous, testosterone-filled muscle men. What she wouldn't give for magical headphones to drown out the thoughts she eavesdropped on, especially because she couldn't turn her ability off when she needed to most. *Luscious hunks from the forces here for training, probably for a quick lay for the week. Work hard, play harder.* There was no way these perfect specimens of virility would have any interest in her. The island, she was sure, would be filled with beautiful women they could pick and choose from, and that would be the end of it. Their internal lust had to have been momentary. She'd been the only woman in the room, and, in absence of any other females, the math worked in her favor. Besides, she wasn't here to get laid, she was here to heal and get a grip on her unmanageable abilities.

Trinity reached the reception desk to find a short line. She took her place at the end and waited. Three attractive ladies crowded around the desk, speaking to a woman with fire engine-red hair, who sat in the chair and flipped playing cards.

"Who made these arrangements with you? I didn't take this reservation." The woman narrowed her eyes at the trio of women making up the short line. Their curly locks of blonde, copper, and brunette fell to above their waists. *These three would catch the sailors' eyes without a doubt.*

"We spoke with a woman. Not sure who she was." The brunette flashed a mischievous grin over her shoulder at Trinity then returned her attention to the receptionist.

"All right, everything you need is here. Your classes for the week, all booked together. You're in rooms four, five, and seven. Take elevator number two, only. Be sure to come down on time for dinner."

"We are gratified with your assistance," the blonde replied. They strolled off to the elevators. The sassy redhead pushed the button.

Trinity readied herself to approach the desk, and the woman held up a finger. "One moment please, miss."

"Sure."

The receptionist walked to a door behind the desk and stepped into the room. Words were somewhat muffled, until Trinity overheard a brief raise in volume. "Who are they?"

"Sisters," another woman's voice replied, irritation tinging her voice.

"I saw something dark in the cards, but it was blocked. I've got a bad feeling about this," the receptionist said.

"We need to tell Rekkus," the second woman ordered. "He'll be back in a few minutes. Talk to him when he's done at the portal."

While the back office debate went on, the trio of women gathered at the elevator whispered to each other. They glanced in Trinity's direction and giggled like schoolgirls. Each had high cheekbones, eyes dark as night, and the perfect features cover models would kill for. Their spilling cleavage bested any competition that would vie for the attention of any man or living creature on the island this week. Just when Trinity didn't think it possible to feel any worse about herself, they proved her wrong. These women were magnificent. She hated them.

Trinity tried to push the internal rumblings of insecurity in her head away. How could it be she was able to read everyone's thoughts on this island, except these rude women? Even worse, why did she care? On a good day, Trinity wouldn't have given it a second thought, but their bad-mannered stares and giggling haunted her. A dark veil shrouded them from her acute perceptions. The lack of perception proved a new experience for her—one she had always fantasized to be a blessing—but her wish had quickly been proven wrong. This circumstance befuddled her, and their incessant stares and laughter annoyed her. What in the world could she have done to warrant such catty behavior? Was it her white hair, or perhaps her rose-colored glasses? The elevator dinged, and they crowded into the box, much to her relief.

"I can help you now." The lady at the desk waved her over.

Trinity approached and peeked at her name tag. She scrunched her nose with confusion. "You're not Cemil?"

"Oh goodness, no. It's the only name tag I could find today. I'm Myron, and you are Trinity McWraith."

She nodded.

Myron flipped another card. "You're well named, for sure."

"What do you mean?"

"Trinity? You're surrounded by the number three."

"I am?"

"You are. In fact, you're a triple threat."

The words stung a little. "What do you mean?"

"Smart, beautiful, and funny. Those guys don't stand a chance in your presence."

"Oh." *What guys? And beautiful?* With stark-white hair, pale skin, and a bit more buxom than the average para woman, Trinity never viewed herself as beautiful.

Her uncle had argued against her view every time he tried to encourage her to get out and find herself a mate. The one thing he didn't want was for her to find another banshee. He went as far as to outright forbid it but never explained why. She avoided men in general. The only person she'd allowed herself to care for since her parents died was her uncle, and even he had met a brutal and untimely demise. Her life experience had taught her the ones she loved would die a horrible death and she was cursed to foresee it. Besides, she was no siren—her talents didn't include timeless beauty which lured men to her bed or their deaths. Trinity shuddered at the thought of romance.

The redhead flipped another card. "Oh, my...." Her brows puckered and distress filled her eyes. "This won't do, not at all," she mumbled. "Sarka will see you in her office."

Trinity bit her lip. "I've only been here five minutes. I couldn't possibly have done something wrong yet." Then, she recalled her awkward arrival and a wave of regret shot through her stomach. "My mistake. Where is she?"

"Right through this door, follow me."

Although the receptionist tapped her foot with impatience while she waited at the door, Trinity didn't rush to see the curt oldest sister who'd snubbed her before she even had a chance to introduce herself. This sister chose not to arrive at all for the sibs' first therapy session, which sent a very clear message of how much she valued Trinity's professional services. She'd heard plenty about Sarka's edgy side and dark demeanor, a bold contrast to her two more gentle siblings who persisted to find resolution with their grief.

"Come in. Please, have a seat." The woman at the far end of the room stood with her back to them. Her sultry voice carried through the office.

"Sarka, I'm going to find Rekkus...right now." The receptionist's tone held discreet urgency.

Trinity glanced at her, reading the hidden blanket of concern shrouding Myron. "Are you okay?"

"Fine, just some business to tend to." She lifted her chin.

Trinity faced Sarka, whose silky waist-length raven hair and black attire created quite a dark appearance.

The woman spun toward her.

"If you'll excuse me?" Myron offered

"Certainly."

When Sarka caught Myron's attention, her neutral expression morphed into a grimace. "He's in the portal room."

Myron rushed out of the office, leaving Trinity to face Sarka alone.

"I'm sorry about my arrival," she blathered and plopped into the wooden office chair in front of the desk.

"The portal is different for everyone. Those clumsy ogres should have been better prepared for you. It's not your fault." Sarka settled behind the desk.

"Oh?" Her unexpected response loosened some of the tension in Trinity's shoulders.

"Cyrus and I met with Cemil and Sage. We discussed the best use of our facilities for your needs."

"Come again?" Caution spiked up her spine. "Which needs would those be?" Her inability to read Sarka's emotion, short of cold, made her uneasy.

"Your circumstances are a little different than

many paras who come here."

"How?"

"You always start without me?" A tall, dark stranger strutted in the door. *Those* piercing eyes Trinity recognized. Dressed all in black, with short dark hair, bronzed skin, and icy-blue eyes stood the fourth sibling. He never left the island, a fact she'd learned all about in her sessions with Sage and Cemil.

"You must be Cyrus." She held her hand out but glanced at the gloves he wore, and withdrew the friendly gesture. "Right...you don't like to touch." Her discomfort grew when she noted his similar demeanor to his sister's.

"We discussed your talents and how overwhelming this island could prove to be for you, unless we put some precautions in place for your well-being." He grabbed a folding chair from the back of the office, and set it down beside his sister, and took a seat across from Trinity.

"Are you gonna lock me up?" She hunched her shoulders. Surely, the crash landing hadn't been so tragic....

Sarka scrunched her nose and narrowed her eyes. "Not at all. We have many guests, both human and para, all with their troubles, emotions, and traumas. We need to make sure we don't put you in harm's way, or, for lack of better phrase, empathic overload."

The phrase struck a chord and then, to her relief, she realized she couldn't see their auras. "Oh, I wanted to thank you for the glasses, Sarka."

"No problem." The ebony beauty waved off the gesture.

Sage sauntered into the room and sat down beside Trinity. "Good evening." She grinned. "We have less-populated cabins by the water. They're more spread out than the rooms here in the Haus. The distance from the energies of the other guests will give you a little tranquility.

"The one exception we cannot waver on is the expectation to join everyone for dinner each night," Cyrus affirmed with a stern glare. "It's the one way we can make sure everyone is accounted for."

"Sage will do some herbal work with you and, before we even consider massage, we will start hydrotherapy, as water will neutralize the negative side-effects you might experience while you heal," Sarka interjected.

"Okay." Trinity waited for the bomb to drop. Although the two dark ones were difficult to read, she could sense they treaded carefully with her. She glanced at each of the siblings with distrust. "What are you not telling me?"

Cyrus shot a hardened stare at Sage.

"Go on," she encouraged him. "She needs to hear it."

"What?" Frustration amplified through Trinity.

The oldest brother exhaled a heavy breath and stood. He removed his gloves and held out his palm. "Your mother's wedding band?" He nodded to her right hand.

Trinity gazed down at the white gold Celtic ring and hesitated. "You're a retrocog," she recalled aloud and then shook her head. "But you hate to read objects, especially ones associated with...." A whimper festered in her chest.

"For you, I'll make an exception because Sage and Cemil are convinced it's necessary." He waved his hand, edginess tinging his voice.

Trinity stared at her ring finger. She knew the object housed horrific pain. If Cyrus read it, she would likely feel his reactions. Coupled with her searing memories of those two fateful nights everyone she loved was butchered, Trinity doubted she could handle much more. Against her better judgment, she tugged the ring off and placed it in his palm. It would be a roll of the dice, since her perceptions were skewed. Sometimes, they were overloaded, as Sarka mentioned, and other times, she couldn't make them work for the life of her.

Cyrus cupped his second hand over the first as he read her ring. He winced and recoiled, his eyes squinted shut, and sucked in a shuddering breath. "Part of the problem you have is you can't control your second side."

She reeled with astonishment. "What do you mean second side?"

"You're part banshee."

"I am a banshee. What is this business about part?" She shrugged with annoyance.

He cocked his head. "You're part empath."

"Empath?"

Sage nodded. "It's why you can read people as deeply as you do."

"Did you not know your mother was half empath?" Cyrus asked.

She sucked in a sharp breath as her chest tightened. "No."

"That's why the banshee drove her crazy. She suffered the grief of all the deaths she called for; it pushed her over the edge." Cyrus clenched his teeth and quickly handed the ring over to her, clearly shaken. "But there's a great deal I can't see."

Sage jumped up and hustled to the counter at the back of the office where she poured a cup of tea then brought it to her brother.

Trinity's mouth grew dry with shock.

"You were right, Sage." He let out a heavy exhale. "She has no idea."

"Best to tear the Band-Aid off, brother." Sarka folded her arms across her chest.

"There's more?" Trinity gripped the armrests of the chair and braced for impact.

Cyrus put his gloves back on. "Your family wasn't murdered by humans, I'm afraid."

"Of course they were. They slaughtered my parents because . we were banshee. They had called for the deaths of their loved ones over the years. I saw them, their necks...." The gruesome images sliced through her brain.

"I'm sorry, but you saw the aftermath of a murder-suicide."

His words pierced her heart. "No!" She shook her head. "Mother never would have—"

"Your father knew she had lost her mind. He had his brother take you out of the house after he had foreseen what was to come. Your mother gave the banshee cry, not only for his death, but her own, too."

Numbness washed over every muscle of her body. "Are you saying because I'm part empath and banshee, I'm going crazy like my mother did? Is this what's happening to me right now?"

"That's not what I meant. Your stress is legit, and the death of your uncle has triggered—"

"Never mind. I don't want to know," she snapped.

Deep down, she knew she had blocked a great deal of trauma after she fled her uncle's grasp and bolted into her family home. What she found, she could never un-see, no matter how hard she'd tried over the years. At the ripe young age of six, Trinity had cried out for both their deaths the night before they perished. Tears of blood had streaked her face. Her mother tried to convince her she'd only had a bad dream, but the next day proved her mother had lied.

"This is a lot to take in right now. Cemil has some

ideas to better work through the rest." Sage stood and coaxed her to her feet. "For now, let's get you to your cabin, we have a little time to get you settled in before dinner."

"Sorry to interrupt, Cyrus." Myron popped her head into the doorway, a frown marring her pretty features.

"What is it?"

"It would seem there's a plumbing issue in some of the guests' bathrooms."

Cyrus cocked his head. "What kind of plumbing issue?"

"We have a bit of a flood on the second floor," Myron blurted. "I've got the property manager, Geoff, on it right now. He'll report back to you when he gets an idea of the cause, but I thought you should know."

Chapter Two

S age parked the golf cart beside a second one at the end of the dock.

"Thanks for seeing me to my cabin." Trinity climbed out, collected her bag, and turned to survey the unique triangular structure at the end of the wooden walkway. Incredible. Built over the water, the villa showcased tall, broad windows all around.

"My pleasure. It's the least we could do." Sage hummed a tune as they walked the length of the boards. "Water will be your number one resource, so what better place than here?"

"I suppose." She spilled out a shaky breath. "How long has Cyrus had to wear those gloves?"

"Since he discovered his talents," Sage replied. "By the time he was twenty-seven, he was a wreck. He couldn't eat or sleep and was haunted by the memories of the objects he read. Every murder, weapon, and unimaginable details of crimes he'd never wanted to see." Sage frowned.

"I guess it would be sort of similar to the dark pit of despair I managed to fall into?"

"I'd say so."

"So he wears gloves to avoid physical contact?"

"It is. Self-preservation for paras can come in

many forms."

"I suppose it does." Trinity fidgeted with her new glasses.

"We had a difficult meeting. Are you okay? You've been quiet since we left the Wiccan Haus."

"I'm fine," she mumbled. "I've lost my mind, and apparently it's genetic. I'm peachy."

"You haven't lost your mind."

"Not yet." The sudden return of Sage's cheery disposition grated on her rankled nerves. "Please don't take this the wrong way. I know you mean well, but I think I would prefer to be alone for a little while."

"Most definitely."

They stepped onto the porch, and Sage opened the door for her. "Dinner is in an hour. Don't be late or Rekkus will send a search party for you. He takes the dinner attendance very seriously."

"So I heard, loud and clear."

"I've set up the bathroom and bedroom with everything you need to relax. The villa can accommodate three people comfortably, with a pull-out couch and the bed, but you have it all to yourself this week."

Trinity bit her lip. "Three people? I don't want to put anyone out with all this business."

"Not in the least."

"Thanks, sorry I'm a little bitchy." Trinity placed her suitcase on the floor by the door as she spun around and soaked up the spectacular room.

Soft pastel colors glinted under the bright beams of sunlight peering in through the windows all around. Furnished with a plush crimson couch set and wooden coffee table on the right side of the entrance, a small circular glass dining table with four chairs in the far corner to the left, and a kitchen with wooden cabinets and a breakfast bar with three stools in the center. It offered luxury at its finest, for a banshee on the brink of madness. A rectangular glass window in the floor even offered a magnificent view of fish swimming under the villa. To the right was the bedroom with a massive king-sized bed covered in lavish white linens she wanted to dive right into.

"This is incredible."

"See, your mood has already lifted." Sage grabbed the door handle. "Myron suggested you take a quick dip in the hot springs before you come to dinner at the Haus."

The idea sparked a little intrigue. "Where can I find it?"

"There's a map on the dining room table. It's a twenty minute walk northwest if you follow the path, but the second golf cart at the end of the dock is for your use. Bring a towel. Myron said you'll need it." She winked and shut the door behind her.

A hot spring? She picked up the map and glanced at it. A hop, skip, and a jump away, it appeared simple enough. Although the appeal of the heated escape could cause her to lose track of time, determination to sneak at least a short swim in before dinner took hold.

Trinity snatched up her suitcase and took it to the bed. She paused to peer out the vast windows at the deep-blue water surrounding her accommodations. She had to hand it to the Rowans. They were a class act. The villa had appeared small from the outside, but on the inside, it offered plenty of space and lush interior, even down to the framed watercolor paintings of beautiful scenery. The place held a serenity she had long since coveted.

She fished through her disheveled clothing, on a mission to find her bathing suit and a summer dress she could switch into and head to dinner afterward. Flustered when she couldn't locate the suit, she emptied her crumpled clothes onto the bed.

"I swear I packed my blue bathing suit," she growled with irritation. "It's not in here." In recent weeks, she had developed a habit of misplacing things and cursed her stupidity. She grabbed the folded note from her pocket and checked it again. In a desperate need to cure her newfound forgetfulness, she had taken to writing lists. Every item she added, she'd crossed off as she packed it in her bag. The suit in question had been third on her list and crossed off. She had, in fact, remembered placing it in the suitcase. She shook her head with despair, and then remembered her spectacular arrival. "It probably got lost when my suitcase burst open on impact with Mr. Hot and Bothered Dark Eyes."

Dumbfounded, she grabbed the sundress, quickly changed, and slipped on her sandals. She snatched a large terrycloth towel from the bathroom and checked her hair in the mirror. "What the...?" After her crash and burn upon arrival, she never had the chance to tidy her do. Taking a quick jaunt to the bed, she snagged her brush and smoothed her hair back into a neat bun. Satisfied, she picked up the towel and headed out the door.

At the end of the dock, she hopped into the golf cart and took a left to follow the trail to her watery retreat. With no suit, she might have to settle for going in only knee-deep, but, for now, she could scout it out. Maybe the Wiccan Haus had a gift shop where she could purchase another one later, or perhaps they'd found hers after she scurried out in such a frenzy.

Upon her arrival, she stared in awe at the magnificence of the steaming spring. Tucked back in the far corner, a light waterfall spray promised a delightful retreat. She spotted flat stones around the edges under the surface of the springs. Were they underwater seats? Nice. She headed to the far side where a stone bench sat beside the waterfall. The humidity settled around her like a warm, cozy blanket. The subtle aroma of mint from the green foliage around the perimeter of the steamy bath soothed her lungs. Trinity slipped her shoes off and set the towel down.

She had the entire hot spring to herself. An impish whim took hold, and she removed her glasses, set them down then pulled her sundress over her head and inched her panties off. She placed all her items on the bench and headed into the water. Skinny dipping had not been her intention, but, hell, the opportunity was too good to pass up.

The water proved even more blissful than promised, a tad warmer than body temperature. She swam around a few laps then set course toward the natural shower. Under the spray, she let the falling coolness wash away her worries, anger, and sorrow. Sarka was a smart lady, suggesting the natural waters could neutralize the negativity festering deep inside, and, by the gods, it worked.

Lost in the tranquility of her shower, she allowed her lids to close as she indulged in serenity. A loud splash startled her, and she opened her eyes. A second splatter sounded, and she crossed her arms over her exposed breasts. The waterfall tucked in the back corner offered little shelter from potential prying eyes. Two heads bobbed across the spring. Dammit. Other swimmers, and here she waded in all her glory, buck naked!

Mortified and now trapped, she held her breath and prayed they wouldn't notice her.

"Man, my shoulders are killing me," one groaned.

"Your shoulders? My back," the other one growled.

The first one dove under the water and disappeared; the second one followed. Her heart pummeled against her ribs as she searched for them. Cautious, Trinity inched forward into the open pool. They hadn't resurfaced for several seconds. Did they both drown?

Right in front of her, a head popped out of the water, and she gasped. *By the gods, it's the two tall, dark, and delicious men I crash landed into at the portal! Could this possibly get any more embarrassing?*

"Shit, I'm so sorry. I didn't realize anyone was in here." His slick black hair glistened with water and the most incredible dark-gray eyes gazed at her.

A second head popped up beside him. "Oh, wow...." He jammed his fingers through his mass of wet locks. She had guessed right—dark-auburn hair and bright-emerald eyes.

"And...this would be the second most awkward moment of the day." She exhaled a shallow breath and sank lower into the water to cover herself. "I think this trumps my arrival."

"Don't sweat it, sweetheart. We'll swim over there," the dark haired one offered, but remained in place with an ear-to-ear grin.

"Yeah, way over there," the ginger concurred, but he, too, didn't budge an inch.

Both men beamed as they treaded water. The dark-eyed hunk's grin held a mischievous quality, whereas green eyes' cheeks flushed bright red. It appeared he was the modest one, at least compared to his counterpart.

She couldn't feel their emotions or read their thoughts. *It must be the water, neutral territory.*

"Arawn, right?" Her teeth chattered. A little too long under the shower, or perhaps the vulnerability of her nakedness in front of two sexy men, set every one of her nerve endings on fire.

"Right," the dark haired one replied. "And this is—"

"Kane," she finished. "The one I didn't knock to the ground."

"Maybe next time." Kane snickered. "You're Trinity."

"Last time I checked." Awkward silence blanketed the hot spring as she waited. "We're late for dinner, I'm sure," she hinted with her arms still wrapped around her goodies underwater.

"Dinner." Arawn licked his lips. "Perhaps you could join us?"

"I...." Temptation niggled at her, but she resisted. "I don't think that's a good idea." To bite her tongue would have been less painful than the moment she declined his invitation. "But thank you."

"Oh?" He frowned. "Sure, we understand."

"Maybe another time?" Kane eased back in the water. "Come on, we should get going," he called to his buddy and swam away.

"See you later." Arawn paused, the depth of his stare captivating her. "Our apologies for the intrusion." He twisted around then dove under the water toward his friend, providing Trinity with a delicious view of his ass, taut and defined, like she'd imagined. So it would seem she hadn't been the only one enticed by the thought of skinny dipping.

When the men stepped out of the water, she tilted her head and watched as she nibbled on her lower lip. They were built like Greek gods, with broad shoulders, rippled arms, and lean hips. She caught a glimpse of their distended cocks, and her breath hitched. They both had a great deal to offer a girl. Tribal tattoos painted the magnificent physique of the dark one, from neck to waist, and over the upper portion of his incredible arms. They were too far away to make out the images, but she couldn't stop herself from the eye-candy overload. The ginger had some remarkable ink, too, covering the width of his back, too, and some across his biceps and chest. Oh Hades, the space between her thighs heated with intensity.

While they got dressed on the other side of the spring, Trinity snuck out to get her clothes. Only, when she got to the bench, all that remained were her glasses, shoes, and her towel. "Are you kidding me?"

Fuming with annoyance, she wrapped the towel around her and stormed to the men. "Very funny, now give me back my clothes," she snarled.

Arawn turned around, his jeans still undone. "Excuse me?"

"I'm not kidding. Where are my dress and panties?" She hugged herself in a vain attempt to ward off the chills of humiliation.

"We didn't touch your stuff, I swear." Kane slipped his T-shirt over his head and inched it down his taut, wet skin.

"Sure you didn't," she growled. "I was here all alone, I put my things on the bench, and you two hooligans showed up. Now, they're gone. Coincidence? I think not." Her cheeks burned.

The guys stared at each other with utter surprise, and then Arawn glared at her. "Hey, we came in from over here. This is where our stuff was, where we entered and exited. Where were your clothes?"

The defensive anger festering in his chest amplified through her. He told the truth.

Trinity's stomach tensed, and she shook her head

in confusion. "Over there." She pointed to the empty surface. "On the bench."

"I swear to you, Trinity, we had nothing to do with it." Kane's words were softer than his buddy's. Trinity absorbed his shock and dismay. Out of the water, they were open books. He told the truth, too.

"I don't understand." She trembled with cold.

"The good news is, you have a towel." Arawn's glare lightened. "You look like you're freezing." He grabbed his T-shirt from the ground and held it up for her. "Use this. We can walk you back to your room so you can get some clothes."

"I couldn't." Her teeth chattered.

"I didn't intend it as an offer." He smirked. "We didn't touch your stuff, but, to be honest, I wouldn't feel right to let you walk back to the Haus in a towel. Whoever took your clothes is probably still around here somewhere."

Fear speared her chest like a dagger, his pangs of concern rippling through her. It had never occurred to her there could be any danger. "I'm in a cabin at the end of the dock, not at the Haus."

"It's settled, then. You've earned yourself a private escort," Kane insisted.

She accepted their offer, and Arawn placed the neck of the shirt over her head and helped her slip her arms in. He inched it down over her towel. Trinity glanced up at his striking charcoal eyes and drank in the warmth of his gaze. Lost in the depths of his incredible orbs, she shuddered as she realized she gazed at their true colors and auras. She felt more naked than she had without a towel. "My glasses." She clasped her hand over her mouth.

"I'll get them." Kane bolted toward the bench and returned with them. "Looks like they left your sandals, too." He kneeled down and, as he held them in place for her to slip each foot into, he glanced up at her with an adoring smile.

Warmth curled around her spine from his tender gaze. *Oh my, this is dangerous territory.* "Thank you, both of you."

Arawn took the driver's seat, and Kane helped her into the passenger. He hopped onto the back of the little buggy, and, within a few minutes, they reached her cabin.

"I don't want to make you late for dinner. You could get in trouble with the boss man."

They walked on either side of her for the quick jaunt along the dock. The heat of their auras extended around her like a snuggly layer.

"Consider it informal security detail. I'll explain to Rekkus. He would expect no less, given the circumstances."

"Since you mentioned dinner"—Kane glanced sideways at her with a roguish grin—"is there a reason you didn't want to join us?"

Trinity's stomach dropped at the question. *How do I respond? You're both too damn sexy for my own good? I'm grieving the tragic death of my uncle and don't want to bore you with the details? Or how about, I'm losing my mind and could become a homicidal maniac at any moment, so your safest bet is to stay the hell away from me. What am I supposed to say?* "I'm, uh...."

"We aren't so bad, are we?" Arawn teased.

"I'm, shy."

"We don't bite." Kane chuckled.

"Unless you want us to." Arawn gazed at her and winked.

These men crept through her defensive shield in a dark, sensual, and very dangerous manner. Despite her best efforts to convince herself there was no way they would be interested in her in the least, here they were, their moderate flirtations and protectiveness comforting her in an unexpected way. They had no way to know she could read their thoughts, and, by the gods, the thoughts they had about her...both of them...together. Worse yet, she liked it.

They reached the porch of the cabin, and her vulnerability burrowed even further inside. "I'll run in and change."

"If you don't mind"—Arawn held her wrist and stopped her—"we should take a look around inside to make sure the cabin is empty."

Trinity sighed. His caution was red hot and not a ruse. "Suit yourselves."

She nodded, and he entered the cabin. Kane stood at her side. Two personal bodyguards. Could this day get any stranger?

A moment later, he returned. "It's clear. Go on in. We'll wait out here for you." Arawn stepped out and held the door for her.

"Thanks, I'll be a minute." She smoothed her wet hair, her bun unkempt again. "And you can have your T-shirt back."

She forced her gaze from Arawn's taut, bronzed flesh and sucked in a shivering breath. *Please cover your body before I'm forced to jump your bones right here on the porch. May the gods have mercy on me.*

Chapter Three

A rawn tried to rationalize the missing clothes as a silly prank some guests may have played on Trinity, but it was more than a game. He felt it in his immortal bones—after all, he had a sixth sense for malevolence. It was a quality he was inherently drawn to, despite the ramifications it usually brought with it. The potential of danger for Trinity was real, so Arawn sped the golf cart along the path to get her to the safety of the Wiccan Haus. But when they arrived, he found himself disappointed because it meant the end of her sitting at his side. The dark edge of his lineage he worked so hard to suppress always managed to surface when something he wanted or, better yet, coveted was within his reach. And he wanted Trinity so badly he could taste it.

"I appreciate how you both took such good care of me and made sure I'm safe and all, but maybe I should ask to be relocated here?" Kane held the door open for her.

"We'll touch base with Rekkus and see what he thinks before we inconvenience you." Arawn placed his palm on the small of her back and escorted her inside. A tingle of arousal shimmied down his spine, like their first encounter when she landed on top of him. It took every ounce of self-discipline not to lower his palm to her lovely heart-shaped ass. Hell, it took everything he had not to devour her luscious lips and claim her for himself, right then and there. The bounce he admired from behind, the sensual swing of her voluptuous hips made his cock strain against the front of his pants. The thin cotton dress clinging to her gorgeous curves offered a flimsy barrier he hungered to tear off.

It wasn't any easier to view her from the front. Creamy mounds peeking out of a dress cut low enough to make his mouth water. She had an exotic oval face with electric-blue eyes, or so he recalled from the brief interaction without her rose colored glasses. The only thing left to his imagination was how long her flaxen locks would dangle if she let them down from the tight bun pinned up on her head. It seemed kind of an uptight do for such a gorgeous creature, but he would work his imagination to its limit for the time being.

Although women threw themselves at him on a regular basis, both para and human alike, he rarely indulged. Despite his extreme libido, few caught his attention, and even fewer managed to retain it. Regardless of his evil heritage, chasing tail for the mere goal of getting his rocks off wasn't a pastime he was inclined to pursue. However, this woman? This incredible creature awakened something so deep and primal inside him, it set every nerve ending ablaze with desire.

Anticipation raked across his muscles like an earthquake. He licked his lips and shook his head to dispel the lust clouding his focus. Something was wrong on the island. He could feel it deep in his gut, and whatever it was, it centered on her. A demigod raised by the Lord of the Underworld, he'd spent enough time around malevolent energy to sense its presence, no matter how minute.

"Myron." Kane approached the front desk.

"Good afternoon." She grinned and flipped her cards. "Rekkus and Cyrus are in the office and would like to speak with the three of you."

"Again?" Trinity moaned. "It's like I'm back in high school, sent to the principal's office over and over." She tsked.

Kane led the way into the back room, Trinity followed, and Arawn trailed after them as he indulged further in the delectable view from behind. *Stop looking at her, you fool!* He gnawed on the inside of his cheek—a vain attempt to ward off his insatiable longing for her. *Damn, I wish I could focus on the matter at hand and not fantasize about my hand on her matter!* He clenched his fists tight and gritted his teeth. *Concentrate on Rekkus. He'll kick my ass to attention.*

"Trinity." Cyrus stood beside Rekkus, their trainer, also the head of security for the island.

Their flexed jaw muscles confirmed his instincts about danger. At least this had been his experience with them being tense and on alert when the island had been invaded by the mob of angry sirens years back.

"I swear I didn't crash into anyone this time." She pouted.

"Of course not. We found something." Rekkus glanced at Cyrus.

"My bathing suit?" Her delicate features lit up with hopefulness.

Arawn prayed the suit hadn't shown up. Although she had cupped her hands over her breasts in the water before he got a good look, she wasn't able to conceal all of her sweetly curved flesh. His cock stiffened at the very thought of her naked, once again. Another dip in the hot springs, sans clothing, was called for in their near future—or so he hoped.

"No." Cyrus waved for her to sit down.

"Kane and Arawn, we've changed your accommodations from the barracks."

"To where?" Panic rushed through him. "Please tell me we are not in the kennels again?"

"No, it's not an initiation, this time." Rekkus smirked.

What a relief. The week he'd made them bunk down with the shifter teens had been brutal at best. No sleep for the entire stay and a throbbing headache from all the howling.

Cyrus cleared his throat, his stern glare settled on Trinity. "We have a security issue and are monitoring the situation. We need these two to bunk with you this week."

"Wait, what?" Arawn choked. *Did I win the karmic lottery or hit the jackpot in abstaining torture?*

"Excuse me?" she sputtered. "What the hell is this?" The flaxen beauty backed away, horror filling her face.

"There is a pull-out bed in your cabin. This is not intended as an intrusion, but, until we get a clearer sense of what this is all about, we are concerned for your safety." Rekkus spoke through gritted teeth.

"I need something more concrete, thank you very much," she snapped. "I didn't agree to come here to play house with men I don't know."

"Trinity?" Sage strolled to them and linked arms with her. "Come with me. These guys are the security gurus of the island. We can chat about some other stuff and leave the drab details to them."

Trinity remained frozen on the spot, speechless, with her mouth ajar and her eyes wide.

"It's okay. I have something to help settle your nerves. We can talk a little about what's transpired today." Sage urged her out of the room, with no more resistance.

Although he hadn't known her long, Arawn had discovered Trinity possessed a spunky streak. If she was unhappy, she quickly voiced it. Just like the verbal lashing she'd bestowed upon him and Kane at the hot springs when she was convinced they took her clothes. She had guts to blast two large men in nothing but a towel. But Sage had grown accustomed in how to tame the wildest beasts on the island, and a panicked woman was definitely within her realm of soothing capabilities.

"What's going on?" He kept his voice low as he closed the door after the ladies left.

"We aren't entirely sure, but it has to do with her." Cyrus exhaled a heavy breath.

"I felt it, too," Arawn concurred. "Tell us what you suspect."

"We can't get a clear read on it. Myron picked up concerned vibes from some women who arrived and some serious danger around Trinity, but we'll be damned if we can figure anything out?" Rekkus grunted with aggravation. "Something is wrong with plumbing on the second floor, and now the heating and cooling system. Who knows what else will go wrong this week?"

"Does Cemil have any idea?" Kane took a chair and plopped down at the desk. "Has he sensed anything about these women?" Arawn joined him. Rekkus and Cyrus did, too.

"Not yet. He was on the other side of the island with a newly-arrived teen. We need to keep the boy away from too much stimulation. Brody has trouble controlling his abilities." Rekkus sighed.

"What kind of abilities?" Kane steeled his back and narrowed his eyes.

"Kinetic." Cyrus grimaced. "Fire, lightning, wind, gravity, you name it."

Arawn tapped his chin. "Would his abilities have anything to do with the plumbing and air systems?"

"I don't think so. The kid has been with Cemil the whole time, hasn't been back to the Haus yet. He will be for dinner, but, so far, he seems to be in good shape." Rekkus shook his head. "The air in this place seems thicker."

"What do you mean?" Arawn studied his expression.

"Intensity or something, the hair on the back of my neck is spiked."

"Your tiger senses?" Kane cracked a grin.

"As a matter of fact"—he curled his lip—"yes."

Arawn fished for more intel. "Has Sarka been able to offer any insights?"

Rekkus snarled at the mention of her name. "She took the reservation. Let's not forget the last time she took a reservation." He growled. "You know how she isn't as careful when she screens guests as Myron is."

Cyrus cleared his throat. "She said they are here for grief work and a power cleanse. They told her they're sisters who'd recently lost their parents."

Kane narrowed his eyes and gritted his teeth. "There's more, isn't there?" His tone dropped an octave.

In the fifty years they'd worked together, Arawn had grown accustomed to Kane's laid-back personality. His buddy wasn't the uptight kind of immortal, so when he reacted, Arawn knew something big had rattled him. He patted Kane on the shoulder.

The elder Rowan brother nodded. "Sarka wonders if maybe there is some magical cloak in place, something that covered up the danger, just not completely."

"If we suspect the three women, why don't we exile them from the island?" Kane's cheeks reddened.

"We aren't certain it is them, and, if they do pose a threat to Trinity, we need to learn how and why before we send her home where she'll be even more vulnerable. Nothing has happened to prove anything. Yet." Cyrus grimaced. "As it stands, it's recon and safety first."

Rekkus let out a low growl. "I don't like this. What if someone is after you?" He glared at Cyrus.

"Myron read my cards. She didn't sense any threat around me, Dana, or the babies. For now, it'll have to do." Cyrus patted the tiger on the shoulder. "At this point, one of our guests may be in danger, so this is our priority."

"What do you need us to do, boss?" Arawn hunched forward. The lingering lust he worked to suppress for the flaxen beauty was abruptly subdued, the threat surrounding her shifting him into protective mode.

"We'll put training on hold for now." Rekkus crossed his arms. "I spoke with Kaleb. A Para Elite team is on standby, and he's agreed you can work on the island security this week and take the extra training you came for after this situation is resolved. You're both to stay with her twenty-four hours a day until she leaves, or until we get this figured out and fixed, whichever comes first."

Just try and keep me away from her. Arawn's mind raced with battle scenarios of faceless assailants.

"You got it." Kane agreed.

"Take shifts, one sleeps, one guards," the boss man continued.

"She's gonna be pissed," Kane grumbled.

Cyrus nodded. "Sage is working with her. She has a theory that this might have something to do with the trouble she's experienced the past few weeks."

"What kind of trouble, Cyrus?" Arawn cocked his head. *Man trouble? Does she have a psycho ex after her?* A jealous streak tore through his bones.

"I can't give you details unless she poses a risk to the island. At this point, she's not the dangerous one, but the one who needs to be protected. She's had a rough go this year, and it's taken a toll. It's all I will say for now. If she confides in you, it will be her choice, but until then, it's a need-to-know basis only. She's entitled to her privacy, and that's already been compromised."

"You have our word, she'll be safe." *Even if it takes my last breath to make sure of it.* Arawn stood and tapped Kane on the shoulder.

"It's dinner time. Sage will bring her to sit with you in the dining room. I would prefer she get back to her cabin sooner, rather than later." Rekkus stood to see them out.

"You got it." Kane opened the door.

Back to her cabin, now there's an idea. The pangs of desire resurfaced at lightning speed. *Protection, get your head on straight. She needs to be safe right now.*

"Oh, and you two Romeos." Cyrus's voice held a cautioning tone. "No funny business."

"Yes, sir," they both replied.

I wish I could guarantee my self-control. Trinity has more power over me, than I do over myself.

39

Chapter Four

The herbal tea Sage had Trinity drink before she came to the dinner hall had tasted sweet and aromatic, but now, somehow, it seemed to kick her ass. The pent-up edges of hostility she was sure she was entitled to feel with the news of imminent danger and bunkmates she had not signed up for, had smoothed out magically. Almost walking on air, she glided into the busy dinner hall, guided by her new best friend, the herbal goddess, Sage. The corners of her lips pulled up into an involuntary ear-to-ear grin.

"Gentlemen," Sage called to the two tall, dark, and yummies as they stood to greet them.

"Looks like you went a little overboard on the rosehips and hibiscus again, Sage?" Arawn chuckled and pulled out a chair for Trinity.

"Are you kidding? Her tea is the bomb." Trinity snickered and plopped into the chair.

"It's a light dinner and straight to bed for you, my dear. It's been a hard day." Sage rubbed her arm and twirled around to leave. Arawn returned to his seat across the table, beside Kane.

"Okay." Trinity chuckled. "But only if these two will tuck. Me. In." She slammed her palm on the table and giggled hysterically. "Together! At the same time."

"Whoa, Sage?" Arawn stared over Trinity's head in the direction of her newfound buddy. "What else was in the tea?"

"The usual, relaxation herbs." The muffled voice behind her held a hilarity that made Trinity chuckle even harder.

"Like the one you dosed me with when I had muscle spasms?" Arawn grumbled.

"Like you said," she replied. "Rosehips, hibiscus, skullcap, and maybe some cinnamon for flavor, oh, and a little damiana."

"Which is for?" Kane fired a glare behind Trinity, too.

"Relaxation, depression, anxiety...." Sage listed. "And, it may have a few side effects."

"Such as?" Arawn narrowed his eyes.

Kane grabbed his glass of water and downed it as if dying of thirst.

"That looks tasty." Trinity hummed. "Garçon, bring a round for everyone, on me!" She whooped.

"Uh, it's also known to produce a mild, short-lived euphoric state...and it's a hormone balancer."

Kane choked and spat a mouthful of his drink across the table. "You gave her an aphrodisiac cocktail?"

"Whew!" Trinity flailed her arms and erupted into a deep belly laugh.

"Not the intended use." Sage patted Trinity on the back. "Greens for dinner and get her to sleep."

"Like this?" Arawn called out.

Trinity twisted around and found her tea peddler had strolled toward the door.

"Sing her a lullaby," Sage called back as she left the room.

***

"Lullaby, that's great." Kane wiped the water from his chin with the back of his hand. Then he snagged a napkin to clean the table. "Not sure how much of this I can take," he grumbled to himself, irritation and longing winding through him.

An incapacitated woman he'd been assigned to protect, and one he desired with every fiber of his being—cruelty at its finest. Damn Sage for putting her in this state. Security was paramount. Kane took his assignments to heart, serving with everything he had, willingly putting his life on the line if that's what it took. Protecting the innocent was his birthright, ran thick in his blood. So much so, he'd followed Arawn and joined the Para Elite Forces when they'd fled the Underworld.

But a gorgeous creature who's been dosed with an aphrodisiac leaving her extremely vulnerable to suggestion? Who exactly is Sage trying to punish here? Her nonexistent inhibitions tormented his primordial urges beyond belief. His groin ached, and his chest tightened in her presence. Thanks to Cyrus, he and Arawn had to stay with her twenty-four hours a day—in her cabin, no less. There was only so much willpower a para of his primal temperament possessed, and he was pushing maximum density at this point.

From the moment he spotted Trinity at the portal, shaken and disheveled, she'd proved the most beautiful woman he had ever laid eyes on—and over his hundreds of years, he had witnessed many. She might be modest, but she was no weakling. As much as he felt inclined to protect her, a profound strength inside her amplified her appeal. His innate sense about people—para or human, it made no difference—alerted him if they had even the slightest evil intention. When he encountered a dark motivation of any kind, his shoulder blades automatically spiked with pain, jolting him into protection mode. But not with this exquisite lady.

In her presence, he found unquenchable desire as well as a deep-seated sense of benevolence he rarely came across. Every inch of her screamed purity, kindness, and powerful sexuality to him. Trinity proved to be his own personal form of opium. Addictive to look at, smell, and touch, even if it was a tap on her shoulder. The fear, however, of her inevitable rejection proved a sufficient barrier to keep his need to pursue her at bay.

Truth be told, when she'd blurted she wanted them both to "tuck her in, at the same time," it piqued his curiosity even more. Kane had never shared a woman with Arawn. In fact, he'd never shared a woman at all. It wasn't as though he had a vast array of past experience, thanks to his station in life. No woman had ever stuck around once his "other side" showed up.

The cloud of longing shrouding his weary brain intensified with every creeping thought. *Snap out of it,* he scolded himself. *The moment she finds out what you are, it's game over, anyway. Don't even bother to get your hopes up. You're hideous, and she is divine. Sooner or later, she'll see for herself. Especially because there's danger around her. You can't hide who you are, and a creature of such beauty would never want a monster like you.*

Kane shook off the internal torment and focused on the meal. The occasional clatter of glasses and cutlery echoed throughout the dining hall, along with the odd scrape of chair legs against the floor as people took their seats for dinner. Every table was filled on both the human and para sides. Low chatter of diners created a gentle hum around them.

"Buddy, it's not so bad. At least she's not pissed," Arawn whispered to him.

"We'll see," he mumbled. "There's always the morning after Sage's herbal concoction wear off." *With the assignment at hand, there's a good chance she'll see the real me before long, and pissed won't even be in the vicinity of how she'll feel then. This, I'm sure of.*

The server carried over a tray of filled plates and placed a colorful salad in front of Trinity.

"Dig in, boys." She gripped her fork like a lifesaver then wavered in her seat as she stared at the tip of the prongs with intense fascination. "Pretty."

"You were saying?" Kane flashed a grin of amusement. His self-pity easily dispersed in light of how at peace she seemed in this moment. The anger which festered in her before had disappeared. Maybe Sage's herbal efforts weren't all bad after all.

"For you, gentlemen." The server placed a thick, bloody steak in front of Kane and veal in front of Arawn.

"Thanks." Kane picked up his utensils and hacked into the crimson meat.

"Ew, what are you, a vampire?" Trinity scowled at his dinner.

"No, but I am a true carnivore, through and through. What can I say?" He tucked the juicy morsel into his mouth and chewed slowly while he watched her. *Maybe subtle hints would soften the blow later....*

Trinity lifted her rose-colored glasses and squinted at him with her magnificent blue eyes. "Why do I see stone around you?" She swayed in her seat.

"And wings?"

Kane's stomach bottomed out. He placed his cutlery down and leaned over his plate to whisper. "What do you mean you see stone and wings?" He knew exactly what she meant. What he didn't know was how she could see it.

"And you!" She pointed her index finger at Arawn. "You seem like a decent guy. Why are you filled with war and revenge? You're so conflicted with your good nature. And your tattoos...what are you hiding?" She set her glasses back in place.

Kane glanced to Arawn and found his comrade with widened eyes. Arawn's shock seemed to match his own. *This may be a short assignment, after all.* He grimaced.

"I want to see those tattoos up close, by the way." She giggled then continued in a hushed tone. "I peeked, you know."

"At...?" Kane cracked a one-sided grin. How could this woman terrify and amuse him at the same time?

"Your tattoos, when we were skinny dipping." She muffled a slight squeal. "I saw his bum!" She pointed to Arawn and slammed her palm on the table again in another short-lived fit of amusement.

"How would you know anything about us?" Arawn maintained his inquisitive stare at the loose-lipped beauty. "Well...." He crinkled his brows. "The tattoos are obvious."

"Oh...." She whirled her hand in a dismissive wave. "That's right, you don't know anything about me...or do you?" She fired a cynical glare, first at him then at Arawn.

"Not much." Kane motioned air quotations with his fingers. "Client confidentiality. Talk to us."

This was a chance to delve into why she was here. Her defenses were most certainly down, although shame washed over him at the need to interrogate her in this condition. Man, he couldn't stop staring at her porcelain features and delectable curves. High cheekbones, full ruby-red lips, and milky mounds that teased the trim of her dipped neckline. She was exquisite, although he preferred her in her more lucid state. What he wouldn't give to take off those glasses and gaze longer into the depths of her eyes...take off her dress and gaze at what lay hidden under that. A flashback of her trying to hide her plump breasts at the hot springs prompted a mischievous grin. Kane cleared his throat and tried to push his lustful thoughts aside.

"Hey, get your mind out of the gutter, stud muffin!" she scolded him. "And you, too," she slurred at Arawn.

"I wasn't—" Kane fibbed.

"Anyway"—she shifted in her chair and straightened her posture—"as fate would have it, I've lost my mind."

"I don't understand." Arawn propped his forearms on the table.

"Well, the low-down...." She leaned over and cupped the side of her mouth as she whispered. "I'm not just a banshee like I was led to believe. It would seem I'm a mixed breed, part empath."

"Is that so?" Arawn prodded.

"Cyrus read my mother's ring." She flashed the white gold band on her right hand and continued. "My parents weren't murdered by humans like I thought. My mother went batty and killed my father and then herself."

"I'm so sorry." Kane's throat grew thick at her herbal-induced confession.

In his years of service to the Para Elite Force and training on the island with Rekkus, Kane had heard tales of how avoidant Cyrus read objects, hence his need to wear his black gloves. Especially objects housing such horrific tragedy. It was difficult to fathom he would even touch her ring.

"That's not the worst of it," she hissed. "Her mixed breed drove her insane, and, as of late, it looks like I'm heading down the same path."

"How so?" Kane hunched his shoulders. Aside from being lambasted by Sage's herbal concoction, he had a difficult time imagining this intelligent, sexy lady as anything but perfect.

"I forget things all the time, especially these past few weeks. I lose things constantly. I can't sleep. I have terrible headaches and nightmares, and then there are the waking visions of brutal deaths I can't seem to shut out anymore." She shuddered.

"It's okay." Arawn reached across the table and set his hand over hers. "You don't have to share. It sounds too painful."

"Oh, pish-posh." She waved her hand and blew out of her pressed lips. "It all happened when I was six. I found out the truth today." She shook her head. "But then, Sage gave me some tea, and I feel kinda funky now." Trinity tipped her head side to side with an exaggerated sigh.

Kane and Arawn sat in awkward silence.

I can't believe such a pure soul as Trinity's is housing so much tragedy. I don't sense insanity. Even the presence of mental illness spikes my shoulder blades with potential for danger. I don't get that with her at all. It doesn't make any sense. This can't be right.

"The worst part," she continued, "was six months ago." She propped her left elbow on the table beside of her salad and planted her chin in her palm. Her sensual lips curled downward into a frown.

"What happened six months ago?" Kane couldn't help himself. The need to know infused every atom of his being.

"I cried the tears of blood."

"Excuse me?" Arawn whispered. "What do you mean?"

With an exuberated exhale, she slouched her shoulders. "When a banshee foresees a death, she wails the banshee cry to let people know to prepare to say good-bye to their loved one."

"Do all banshees cry blood?" Kane had heard tales of her breed over the last millennia but never a word about this bizarre twist. The more she shared, the more mystery clouded his perception of her.

"No, that's the whole point. I've only ever cried tears of blood once before, with the pending death of my parents. This time...." Her lower lip quivered. "I foresaw the death of my uncle."

"You did?" Kane's heart sank.

"Yup. For a brief while, I really thought we would be okay if we lived in the human world." She sank back into her seat with a pout.

"Because?" Arawn had pushed his dinner to the side and studied her with dark fascination.

"My uncle refused to let me live in Ireland, among the other banshees or otherwise."

"Why?" Kane cocked his head. *Banshee's come from Ireland. It's strange not to be raised among your own breed.*

"To start with, he was mortal, but my father was a banshee."

"I thought banshees were only women?"

"It's true, males are rare in our race, but my father was one. He and my uncle were half-brothers."

"Why did your uncle refuse to raise you with your race?"

"The little information he shared never seemed to paint the whole picture for me. He said after my parents' deaths, we fled Ireland for safety and the sovereign of the banshee had become corrupt. He honored my mother's final wishes and raised me away from the tribe." She bit her lip and gazed at the table.

"If you couldn't live among your own, what did you do?" Arawn propped his forearms on the table.

"We moved a great deal, every few years, and traveled the world."

"To travel so much...sounds exciting," Arawn prodded.

Trinity pursed her lips. "Not really. Each time we got settled, Uncle Connor would get anxious and pack us up to go. We kept to ourselves mostly."

"Well, it would be hard on a child," Kane agreed.

"Once I got older, I went to college, got my degree, set up the perfect mundane life, and the humans seemed to accept me and didn't ask many questions. They didn't know my history or lineage. My uncle had grown old and frail. I convinced him to stay with me so I could take care of him."

"Then what?" Kane pressed for more, cautious not to overwhelm her.

"We had just come home from a nice dinner out. I glanced at him and his aura turned blood red, I blacked out and when I awoke, he wiped my face with a wet cloth, he was white as a ghost." Trinity wrapped her arms around herself and began to rock back and forth. She fixed her gaze on her plate.

"Did he say anything?" Kane probed.

"He said I screamed so loud, it shattered all the windows in the apartment." She quieted her voice. "And tears of blood streamed from my eyes. He knew what it had meant, and so did I, even if I couldn't remember it."

Kane frowned. *The terror she described.... I wish I could erase the pain for her.*

"What did he know?" Arawn fished for more detail.

"He knew the exact same thing happened before my parents were murdered. I wailed the banshee cry and tears of blood poured down my face. He knew my cry was for him this time."

"Why did you want to live in the mundane world?" Kane spoke softly.

"Many paras knew the tale of my tribe. From what Connor said, we are cursed. I wanted to live in a place where no one knew me and I could start over. I wanted to help people heal. I became a psychologist. I lived in New York, had a nice, mundane life with an apartment on Park Avenue, my practice, and everything I worked so hard for."

"Had?" Kane arched his brows.

"Yeah." She sighed. "I have nothing left to go back to. My patients are all gone...to be honest, I don't have any desire left to help anyone anyway. I'm effectively burnt out."

"I'm sorry to hear that."

A prickle of caution surfaced in his shoulder blades. The first awareness of malice and his wings automatically sprouted out of his flesh, as a rule. But this was minor; something was off. He couldn't detect the direction the hint of dark energy came from, but he sensed the slightest trace of malevolence. Kane drew in a long sniff and glanced about the room as he assessed the risk level. He smelled the different breeds—vampires, shifters of all kinds, and the humans—but none radiated evil. He attuned his enhanced hearing and eavesdropped on the dozens of conversations all happening at once. No mention of

Trinity, and no comments to cause alarm.

Suddenly, she steeled her back and lifted her glasses. She narrowed her eyes and scanned the room. Kane followed her baleful stare to find three women sitting together; they glanced at Trinity and held the most bizarre grins.

"What are you hags staring at?" She let out a venomous hiss.

"Whoa there, sweetheart," Kane hushed her and gripped her flailing hand. "They're other guests, having dinner at a different table, nothing to concern ourselves with." The minute trace he sensed came from no direction, not even from the threesome Trinity had turned her attention to.

"Oh really? I see the hideous faces they think they can hide from us all. I can hear their thoughts, and those bitches make my blood boil." She stood and scowled at them. "You wanna go?" Trinity gritted her teeth and fisted her hand that Kane held tight, her knuckles whitening. "Bring it. I'll wipe the floor with each of you."

A pungent aroma of adrenaline wafted up Kane's nose, the sour scent emanating from Trinity. He was all too familiar with the odor—fear. She felt threatened. *I don't sense a distinct threat. Is she truly losing her mind? Is this what she spoke about minutes ago?*

"Princess, look at me." Arawn stood and rubbed her shoulder. "Tell me what happened to your uncle."

Trinity fixed her gaze on him. She lowered her glasses again, her hand loosened in Kane's grasp, and her posture slumped. Kane released his grip, and she plopped back into her seat and shook her head.

The cutting scent suddenly dispersed, and the prickle in his shoulder blades eased. *What the hell was that?* He studied the room again but found nothing to explain his instinctive reaction to danger.

"I can't." Her chin quivered.

He glanced at the table of women. The trio casually talked amongst themselves and sipped their drinks as if nothing had happened seconds ago. *Bizarre.*

"It's okay," he offered in a soothing tone. "You don't have to."

"No," she lamented. "I mean, I can't. I don't remember anything about that night."

Kane couldn't see clearly through her tinted lenses, but he would bet his life tears threatened to spill down her beautiful face. An urgent need to wrap his arms around her and shield her from sorrow caused a deep ache in his chest, and the conscious decision to refrain from his impulse was almost impossible to adhere to. Their inquisition needed to stop, now. "I'm so sorry for all you've been through."

"I know you are. I can feel it." Trinity glanced at him with a curious grin. "But I'm amazed that you do...with a heart of stone."

Kane held his breath in shock.

"And you, too." She motioned to Arawn. "Why do hounds with red ears hunt you down?"

Chapter Five

The pounding in her head amplified as she battled groggy fatigue. Bright light penetrated her eyelids, and, grabbing a pillow, she hid underneath it. She rolled back and forth, groaning in agony.

"Hey, are you okay, princess?" a raspy voice called out.

Trinity bolted upright, panic racing through her veins. "What the hell?" She grimaced at the sharp pain stabbing her temples. Upon a quick glance around, she found herself in the villa's king-sized bed and spied hunk number one across the cabin, on the pull-out couch.

A brief thump sounded on the roof over her head then a huge thud outside the door.

"What the hell was that?"

"Oh, Kane's up now." Arawn tucked his hands behind his head with a grin.

"Up? From where?" She frantically scanned the room for the ginger.

Arawn pointed to the ceiling. "The rooftop."

"Excuse me?"

Kane opened the front door and strolled in, stretching his arms out with a yawn.

"Why the hell are you two in my cabin?" She grabbed the sheets and pulled them over her chest. "And on my roof?" Suspicion roared through her aching head, and she glanced down, relieved to find she still wore her summer dress. "Oh Hades, what did I do?"

"It's okay." Kane held his palms up in surrender. "Remember, we're your bunkmates this week?"

She glanced to his side where the hunk with dark eyes lay on the couch. Thankfully, they both were still fully clothed. "Mind telling me how in Tartarus I got into the bed?" The blur of the evening horrified her. Minor blackouts had become more common than she cared to admit, recently, but this one was a complete blank slate.

"Yeah, Sage went a little overboard on the...relaxation cocktail last night." Arawn climbed off the couch. He tidied his bedding, folded the pull-out bed, tucked it away and then replaced the cushions. "We brought you back to the cabin and tucked you in. As per your orders, if I do recall correctly." He flashed a sheepish grin.

Dismay washed over her at the recollection of her words in her euphoric state of intoxication. *But only if these two will tuck. Me. In.* "Oh, right." She covered her blazing cheeks with icy palms, desperate to wake up from this humiliating moment.

"If it makes you feel any better...." Arawn's tone was kind but comical. "I've had the same thing happen when I got a charley horse in training a few months back." He rubbed the back of his thigh and shuddered.

"Time for caffeine, I think." Kane headed for the kitchen. "Are you a tea or coffee kind of gal?"

Trinity's pulse raced. How did she manage to get herself into this situation? "Normally, I would say tea, but the way I feel right now, I'll take coffee intravenously if you've got it." She dropped back onto her pillow as the current bunk arrangements slowly came back to her. Right. Cyrus and Rekkus ordered these two to be her personal bodyguards. So much for a week of relaxation. "When Sage dosed you"—she studied Arawn with narrowed eyes—"did you have a hangover?"

"A little." He shrugged. "Felt a little drunk in the morning."

"Is there any aspirin? My head is killing me." She rubbed at the painful throb in her temples.

"I didn't get a headache." He approached her bedside.

"Whoa there, buddy. I don't have any desire to play doctor." Although the thought did hold some appeal, she'd never admit it, especially given how much she hurt.

"Let me check your eyes. No funny business, I swear."

Sensing his genuine concern, she caved. "Fine."

Arawn sat on the edge of the bed and leaned in. His striking charcoal orbs caught and held her attention. Warmth trickled down her solar plexus at the invasion of his tender energy, and then she clasped her hand over her eyes with fright. "Where are my glasses?"

He patted the nightstand. "Right here. You didn't need them while you slept."

She peeked between her fingers, and he flashed a gentle smile.

"May I?" He motioned to her face.

"Yes." His aura held gold and orange, kindness and fierce protectiveness, a vision she could live with for the moment.

He leaned closer and checked her eyes then

55

retreated. "Don't be alarmed, but I want to call Sage."

"Why?"

"Your pupils are severely dilated. I can hardly see any of your spectacular blue." He forced the corners of his mouth back. "Maybe too much of Sage's herbs? It could explain the headache."

"I feel like I got run over by a train," she confessed. "But I've been having these headaches for weeks. This is the worst one yet."

Kane approached them with a steaming cup in his hand. "We're fresh out of IV bags. Hope this is okay."

Trinity sat up and accepted the warm mug.

"I took a guess...double cream, double sugar?" He grinned. "If not, I can make another one." Kane's aura emanated gold and green, another beautiful energy she could handle with ease.

"Sorry, I didn't mean to come across as so bitchy. This is perfect, thanks." She blew against the steamy brew and sipped a mouthful. Sweet and creamy, the taste of perfection. She swallowed, and a hostile reaction took hold. Her stomach churned. "This may not be such a good idea after all." She gripped the cup with disappointment. "Damn, it tasted good."

"It's okay, princess." Arawn patted her hand. "After Sage's herbal roofie, I found myself pretty disoriented, too."

Trinity giggled, and then winced at the sudden escalation of pain in her head.

"We need to get Sage, now." Arawn took her cup and placed it on the table. He eased her back and settled her pillow around her head with gentle movements.

She let her eyelids flutter closed, but it seemed like she'd just drifted off when a knock at the door startled her awake.

Kane opened the door and let Sage and Cemil into

the villa.

"Hey." Cemil took a few steps, and then halted. He gripped Sage's arm and stared at Trinity, his face paling. He cringed and then shook his head. His knuckles whitened around his walkie-talkie.

"What is it?" Sage rubbed his shoulder as lines of concern fanned out from her bright eyes.

Trinity sat up and patted her face then smoothed back her hair. Surely she couldn't be that hideous in the morning? "What's wrong?"

"The pain." Cemil shook his head and shivered.

"It's really bad?" Sage's confusion alarmed Trinity.

"What's going on?" She winced again, agony rippling through her brain, and she dropped back onto her pillow. She grabbed the glasses from her bedside table and eased them on with shaking fingers. "I can't tune anything out."

The siblings approached the bed, and Sage sat at her side.

"Did you overdose her with the herbs?" Arawn stood on the opposite side of the bed, his voice low and serious.

"No, this isn't herbal. Something is wrong." Sage took her hand. "Tell us what you remember."

Trinity searched her foggy brain. "Tea, salad, stone, wings—" She jolted. "My blabbermouth!" Her unfiltered confession whirled through her head. "I never meant to...."

"It's forgotten, don't stress." Kane nodded, his lips pressed tight. "We didn't hear a word, I promise."

No matter how hard she tried, she couldn't block it or push it aside. "I can't take it. You're all afraid, worried for me. It's too much." She curled into the fetal position and wailed. "Please, go away."

"Sage, I need you to have Trixie and Serena meet us at the hot springs, right away," Cemil muttered.

"I'm on it." She jumped up from the bed and snagged the handheld radio from his grasp.

"Arawn, I can't touch her right now. The overload is like a shockwave, and I'm just standing beside her. I need you two to get her to the hot springs, right away."

"You got it." Arawn bent down and scooped her up into his arms.

Cemil held the door open for them. "I'll go meet with Rekkus and Cyrus. There's something big going on here, and we need to figure out what it is.

Chapter Six

Arawn cradled Trinity in the backseat as Kane drove the golf cart. This exquisite creature suffered terribly, and he was powerless to stop it. If he could switch places with her to save her from the pain, he would in a heartbeat.

She clamped her hands on the sides of her head and trembled violently. His heart sank, and his chest ached for her.

"Please, don't worry," she begged.

"Everything will be okay," he hushed her.

"No, I mean stop thinking. I can't take it," she wailed.

"What do I do?" His helplessness amplified.

"Close your eyes. Let your mind empty...." She widened her eyes. "I can't take the worry."

"You've got it, princess." Arawn closed his eyes and worked to still his thoughts. *Impossible. I can't not worry for her.* The more he tried, the harder she shook. "I'm sorry, I'm trying."

Kane pulled to a stop at the hot springs. Arawn planted his feet and rose carefully with her in his arms. At the edge of the water stood Serena, the resident mermaid, and Trixie, the half fae who instructed yoga and relaxation for the guests on the island.

"Get her into the water," Trixie called to them as she waded in.

Serena followed and dove under. She emerged, and a multi-colored fin splashed the surface, replacing the legs she had just walked on.

Arawn carried Trinity into the springs. The heat of the natural pool enveloped him up to his waist. Glancing down at the woman in his arms, the urge to kiss her forehead caught him off guard, as did his need to keep her close.

"You're sweet, but I still can't take it." She peered up at him then cupped his cheek with a shaky hand.

"What?" *The kiss or the caring? I hope to Hades it's not the kiss.*

"You carried me all the way here, and you want to kiss my head, too. It's charming, you big lug."

Arawn grinned. "My pleasure, ma'am." *Thank Hades it's not the thought of a kiss she dreads.*

"We've got her." Trixie and Serena eased her from his grasp.

"Can we stay with her?" he protested.

Kane joined him in the water.

"We've got this." Serena offered a smooth but stern voice. "Besides, Rekkus and Cyrus want to see you both right away."

"But—"

Trinity's hand to his cheek made him hesitate.

"Please, do as she says."

"What will you do with her?" Kane's voice cracked.

"We need to get her relaxed first," Trixie answered in a calm tone.

Serena supported her and guided her as she floated on her back toward the falls. "Close your eyes. Can you feel anymore thoughts right now?"

"No." A tremored giggle erupted from her. "By the

gods, it's stopped."

For the first time since she awoke this morning, she smiled and didn't flinch in pain. Relief washed over Arawn at the magical transformation.

Trixie stepped into his line of sight. "Cemil stopped in before you got here and asked me to do some hypnotherapy. He said she's missing pieces of her memory?"

"From what she...uh...admitted last night"—*in her herbal daze*—"parts about her parents' deaths. She was only six, but she said she can't remember her uncle's death. I don't know anything about it."

Kane cleared his throat. "She said she's forgotten and misplaced things for weeks—headaches, nightmares, waking visions of death. She doesn't understand it." He furrowed his brows. "She thinks she's lost her mind."

"Yeah," Arawn agreed, his buddy having jarred his recall of the details she had disclosed. "She said her mother went crazy and killed Trinity's father and then herself. She said her mother was an empath and banshee, and it drove her mad."

"And," Kane continued. "She couldn't recall anything after dinner in the hall until she woke up this morning."

Trixie's eyes widened. "How long ago?"

"At least two hours before we put her to bed." Arawn's gaze dropped to his floating angel. "She didn't talk much more. She was pretty out of it."

"Thank you both. Your information is very helpful. I need to find out why she has memory loss. It may explain the severe pain and how besieged she is."

His feet sat heavy on the sand like piers of concrete—he had no will to move away from her.

"Will she be okay?" "We'll get her settled, I'm sure she'll be fine. The water seems to have helped already. Go, now." Trixie patted him on the chest. "We'll take good care of her. Once we're finished, we will meet you back at the Haus."

Kane shook his head. "If there is trouble on the island, we can't leave you here alone."

"Cemil has already sent for more security. They're on their way. Hang out at the water's edge until they arrive, but I don't want her to see you right now. We need her complete focus."

Arawn followed Kane to the underwater ledge farthest from where the women worked with Trinity.

They stood in silence as he watched from afar, devastated that the women got to stay with her when he couldn't. They held her and talked to her. The anguish of not being close enough to hear what they said jabbed icicles of bitter envy through his veins. Not a demigod who gave in to the need of prayer, Arawn contemplated any potential benefit to Trinity if he murmured a few words to whichever deity might be listening. Hell, he'd sell his soul back to his own father if it meant saving her, regardless of the endless suffering he knew awaited him there. Days ago, his life was satisfactory, having never known Trinity. Now, the prospect of her not surviving this caused his gut to churn with terror at the very thought of losing her. Although he had an acute need to protect her, she wasn't helpless. The power her slightest smile had on him was mindboggling.

The softest growl from his buddy beside him roused him from his state of self-pity. He had become so consumed with the banshee goddess, he hadn't even paused to consider how Kane felt about the situation. Protecting the innocent was his best friend's genetic coding. As much as Arawn felt like he'd failed her, Kane, for sure, would take the inability to shield her from harm even harder.

"How you doin', partner?" He nudged Kane's arm.

"It's not me I'm worried about." The soft rumble of his buddy rattled him. His friend stood and folded his arms tight across his chest.

It would seem she's managed to get under more than just my skin.

In all their years of friendship and comradery in service, he had never witnessed Kane fixate on any woman except the one human he saved before they joined the force. The same woman who shattered his heart when she screamed bloody murder and ran from him as if he were the devil incarnate.

Once security arrived, Arawn and Kane left the golf cart for the girls and jogged back to the Haus. Arawn appreciated the physical outlet. Tension and worry strained every muscle in his body, despite the cold, wet clothes which clung to his skin from wading into the hot springs with Trinity. The vision of her in so much pain and both of them being so helpless to shield her in any way, traumatized him. It was a far cry from the protection they offered as Para Elite Forces men.

Never in his existence, even in the Underworld, had Arawn felt so powerless as a protector. Even when he crusaded against his namesake, his father, standing for what was right rather than his birthright of war and revenge. The epic battle had been easy as pie compared to this. Then again, in those circumstances, he'd known exactly who the enemies were and could determine what action would readily be needed. He rubbed his sternum as the memories stabbed through his head and straight down to the scars over his chest and arms.

They ran at a moderate pace along the beaten path of the forest. The fresh scent of greenery filled his nose with each inhale. The wind rustled the leaves and the breeze brushed his skin, cooling the beads of perspiration along his face and neck.

"Arawn?" Kane called to him as they jogged.

"Yeah, buddy?"

"You think she's gonna be okay?" Kane slowed his pace and then halted.

Arawn stopped and spun around to face him. He bent over and rubbed his thighs as he caught his breath. "I hope so."

"You're as scared as I am, aren't you?" Kane set his hands on his hips and twisted his upper torso from side to side in long stretches.

"Yeah, I hated to see her in so much pain, it...."

"Broke my heart, too," Kane finished his exact thought.

Arawn took a leap of faith and confided in his best friend. "We both seem to have some strong feelings for her."

Kane nodded. "I can't understand how I managed to fall so hard for her in such a short span of time."

"You and me both, brother." Arawn raked his fingers through his hair. "This is kind of a first for us," he prodded. "If you want me to stay away...?"

"I planned to offer the same thing to you." He cracked a grin. "I mean, if you think she's into your ugly mug."

"Nice." Arawn snorted. His amusement dissipated quickly. "How do you think she'd feel about...?" He couldn't bring himself to entertain the thought, not while she suffered so.

"I think it's fair to say, there's a connection with the three of us, I mean, I can feel it." Kane patted his shoulder. "It's new territory for you and me, for sure. It wouldn't feel right if only one of us had her to ourselves."

"You think she'd be into both of us?" Arawn tilted

his head with surprise. "I mean, she did make the comment about us...."

"Tucking her in together. Yeah. I caught it, too." Kane bit his bottom lip.

The fact this possibility didn't trigger the severe jealous streak he'd experienced earlier at the mere thought the danger could have been an ex of Trinity's baffled him. A bizarre comfort came with the thought of sharing her with Kane. Not Arawn's norm, and he and his buddy were both straight with no inclination toward romance with one another. Share was not a word he used often. Hell, even the suggestion of splitting a meal with the big guy was enough to spark competition between the lifelong friends.

"It's a possibility, but I have to put it out there if there's even a remote chance she might be interested." Kane smirked.

"Go on," he challenged.

"If we ever have a chance to get together with her, it's about her...not...." Kane motioned back and forth between them both.

"Whoa, yeah. That's a given, dude." Arawn grimaced. "Even if I were into guys, which I'm not, let's be clear"—he shuddered at the notion—"I couldn't handle your hideous mug naked." The subtle jab eased some of his tension and brought him to a chuckle.

"To be honest"—Kane's smile faded—"I don't know if I could take the rejection. I've never met anyone like her before."

"She's under my skin, too. I thought being in the forces would reduce the temptation to fall for a woman. Then she landed...right on top of me." Arawn scrubbed his face at the recollection of her arrival in the portal room.

The heat of her body against his, the sweetness of

her breath brushing over his lips. It had taken every ounce of self-control not to claim her as his own, right there in the middle of the floor. The awareness of the boss man, Rekkus, who stood right there, had been the only thing holding him back from his primal impulses.

Neither of them spoke the rest of the way back. The strain on Kane's face at the cabin and the water had been unmistakable. Their talk confirmed it. They had both fallen, hard for this flaxen beauty.

Kane had been by his side since the battle of Annwn and never had Arawn seen him so shaken by another's pain. Something was seriously wrong here, and they both sensed it.

Arawn held the door open to the Haus for his buddy and followed him in.

"Good morning, gentlemen." Myron sat at the front desk and flipped her cards. "They're all in the office, waiting for you."

When they entered the room, Rekkus and Cyrus stood in the corner in deep conversation. Sarka, Cemil, and Sage huddled around the desk. Arawn cleared his throat to announce their presence.

"Come on in. We need to talk." Rekkus waved them over.

"What's the news?" Kane folded his arms over his chest.

"Did you sit watch over the villa last night while she slept, Kane?" Rekkus approached him, his teeth clenched tight.

"I did, from the moment we got her back until after sunrise."

"Did you sense anything out of the ordinary?" Cyrus joined them.

"I can't describe it." Kane paused. "At the dinner hall, there was a hint, for a moment, of something, but I couldn't smell, hear, or see where it came from, and it disappeared as quickly as it showed up. Last night on the rooftop, I saw and heard nothing. Even my radar for dark energy didn't pick up any indication of anything out of the ordinary, but I felt kind of dazed, almost like a daydream."

The fair-haired Rowan brother stepped toward Kane and held out his open palm. "May I?"

"Sure." Kane accepted.

Cemil held his hand and closed his eyes for a moment then sucked in a sharp inhale. "Trance-like?" He opened his eyes and released his grip.

"Yeah, I would say tranced was pretty much how it felt."

"If even *you* couldn't sense anything, we have a serious problem." Rekkus dropped his head back and heaved a sigh layered with frustration. "How are we supposed to protect her?"

"Any theories so far?" Arawn dug deeper. "The humans seem fine." Sarka plunked herself into the office chair and intertwined her fingers. "But there are flooding and air system malfunctions on the second floor, the lighting down here has been flickering, and some of our para guests have reported nausea."

"Food poisoning?" Kane debated.

"No, those who have complained had different menu items." Sage joined her sister. "There is something dark on the island, but none of us can hone in on it."

"The humans are protected, unaffected by all that has transpired, am I correct?" Arawn pondered out loud.

"Yes." Rekkus raked his fingers through his hair. "For now, but if it does begin to affect them, she's off the island."

"Just because you can't see magical creatures doesn't mean they're not there," Arawn offered.

"What kind of creatures do you think they are?" Sage tipped her chin up. "The island is protected. We have every provision in place."

"We thought the same thing before the sirens invaded, too, but every defense could potentially have a weakness," he cautioned the group. "Those desperate enough to get in will do their very best to find a way. Take it from someone who knows. When malevolent beings have an agenda, they always find a way."

"So far, this seems to affect mostly Trinity. Maybe she has lost her mind?" Sarka offered coolly.

"No, she hasn't," Kane growled.

"Easy, big guy." Cemil held his palms up to tame the beast. "This is just a brainstorm right now. We need to weigh all the possibilities."

Arawn tapped his chin in deliberation. "Sarka, is there any way to dull Trinity's senses for the time being?"

"She has the enchanted glasses, but they haven't helped." She shrugged.

"Correct me if I'm wrong, but those dull her *visual* perceptions, right?" he disputed.

"You're right," Cemil's voice livened up. "She's part empath, so she feels everything on all levels."

"What do you propose?" Cyrus lifted a single brow.

"I'm not sure, but the pain she was in at the cabin was surreal, brutal." He shook his head as if to dispel the experience. "Kane, Arawn, has there been a time since you've been with her, she's been at complete peace?"

"You mean outside of the herbal roofie Sage gave her last night?" Kane pressed his lips tight and narrowed his eyes.

"Yes," Cemil retorted.

"The hot springs." Arawn's hopes lifted. "The moment Serena had her submerged in the water, she said she couldn't feel anything. She giggled with relief."

"Well, we can't keep her submerged in water the rest of the week. She's not a mermaid." Cemil frowned, then his eyes lit up. "This may be a shot in the dark, but Sarka, can you fashion a talisman to carry spring water in it?"

"If this is a cloaked being, and with this caliber, there may be more than one, I would bet it's a psychic attack. The water neutralizes negative energy for her, but she needs more than one element. If I fashion a talisman for her out of black tourmaline, perhaps a mini vial with water in it, it can protect her from negative energy, even spells and curses. She can't take it off at all, though, and I can't guarantee how long it will last because we don't know what we're dealing with."

Sage sat on the edge of her chair. "We can amp up the power with some herbs, too. Mugwort can protect against astral attack, since no one can see anything. Acacia is good for psychic attack; black thorn can reverse a spell."

"Okay, you two, work together on the talisman. Cemil, once she's got the protection in place, what other vulnerabilities does she have?" Cyrus inquired.

Cemil straightened his back, determination filling his features. "Unresolved grief."

A knock sounded at the door. Sage pulled the door open a crack, and whispered. Then she let in the tall, silver-haired fae.

"Trixie, you were fast," Sage remarked.

Is this a good sign or not?

The fae entered the room and frowned. "Only

because parts of her memory has been completely erased." She closed the door behind her.

"Where is Trinity?" Kane's nostrils flared.

Trixie held up her right hand. "Serena's still with her. She's helping her balance her emotions in the springs. Two security guys stayed at the water's edge to keep an eye on them."

"What have you learned?" Cyrus's voice lowered.

"Someone has seriously messed with her. I regressed her to last night, and even in her subconscious, she has no memory of a two hour span. Dark shadows surrounding her in the dinner hall were the only things she could recall before her head started to hurt."

"She was pretty out of it," Kane concurred.

"Did anything happen in the hall?" Trixie probed further.

"She told us about her uncle, her parents, and that she's a mixed-breed," Arawn listed as he recalled the events. "She read a little about each of us. She picked up on wings and stone from Kane here, and war and revenge with conflicted nature, and the hounds of hell from me." He rubbed his chest with discomfort.

"But none of those things set her off," Kane disputed. Then his eyes widened. "She got pretty feisty when she read some women's thoughts. Three attractive women together. Redhead, brunette, and a blonde."

"The sisters." Rekkus nodded.

"What thoughts did she pick up on?" Cemil asked.

"She didn't specify, but she said they made her blood boil, and she saw the faces they hid. She would have scrapped with all three of them." Arawn set his hands on his hips. "I distracted her. I should have asked," he grumbled.

"You kept the peace. Nothing about the shape she

was in seemed logical." Kane patted his shoulder. "And the women didn't do anything specific, or at least anything we noticed. They sat at dinner. Then we took her back to the villa."

"There's more, I'm afraid." The tall, slender fae knitted her brows. "The death of her uncle...she was there but has absolutely no memory of the death, the night, or the day after."

Kane crossed his arms. "Isn't that normal with trauma?"

"On a conscious level, yes, but there should be a subconscious recall of some sort."

"But I saw the images," Cemil disputed.

"When?" Arawn twisted to face him.

"The last time we met at her office in New York. I picked up on graphic details, brutal images." Cemil shuddered.

"How did he die?" Kane whispered.

"I didn't see his death, but it was slow, vicious, and painful. I saw the aftermath which haunts her."

"I read the same with her mother's ring for her parents' deaths," Cyrus concurred.

"Look, I can't explain it," Trixie said. "But it's as though she was traumatized by these brutal deaths, and then someone erased the memories completely but left the damage in its wake."

Cemil cupped his chin. "I'll have to take her to the Elysian Fields. She needs at least some closure to resolve her grief."

"Not until after we make the talisman," Sarka spoke up.

"And after some food and another night of sleep. She's exhausted on every level, physically, mentally and emotionally," Cemil finished.

"So, her treatment and protection is sorted out." Cyrus stared him down. "Kane, you continue to sit watch while she sleeps. Arawn, take turns on watch."

"You got it, boss." Arawn's eagerness to get back to their banshee and see for himself she was okay overpowered him.

"There's one piece of the puzzle missing that really bothers me." Rekkus locked gazes with Cyrus. He stepped closer to him.

"I didn't think we had enough pieces to form a puzzle," Sarka sneered. Rekkus glared at her, and she straightened her posture. "What's missing?"

"If someone wants to hurt her, we won't find out whom until we figure out why."

"How do you propose we do that?" Cemil tilted his head.

"I haven't figured it out yet, but I will." Rekkus curled his lip.

"She did mention one thing that seemed odd. She didn't have much information, though," Kane spoke up.

"Go on?" Rekkus nodded.

"She said her uncle took her and fled Ireland after her parents died, and he refused to raise her among her race."

"Did she say why?" Cyrus's eyes widened.

"Not much, but she said he felt the sovereign of the banshee is corrupt. From the way she described her childhood, they moved around a lot, and he was pretty anxious about it."

Chapter Seven

T rinity tossed and turned. As tired as she felt, she couldn't sleep any longer. She threw the covers off and stared at the large round bamboo blades of the ceiling fan. The soft whoosh as it slowly spun did little to lull her restlessness. She gazed aimlessly at the dancing shadows from the blades against the plaster swirls of the butter cream ceiling.

"You okay?" Kane approached the bed, a mug in hand.

"Yeah, I know Trixie told me to sleep, but I'm not tired anymore." She propped up against the hard wood of the headboard. "Is this for me?" She licked her dry lips with anticipation.

"Sure is." He handed it to her. "I just got up, myself. I debated brewing some coffee but went with this instead."

"What is it?" She drew in a long whiff of aromatic sweetness.

"Tea." Kane sat on the bed beside her.

"Tea?" Apprehension rolled over her. "On second thought...." She handed the mug back.

Kane accepted it with a knowing grin. "It's not one of Sage's zany concoctions. It's chamomile I found in the cupboard. See?" He sipped from the cup and let out a low moan of enjoyment. The noise sparked her intrigue...not for tea, but how he would moan with a different kind of pleasure.

Kane held the cup for her to taste.

"Thank you." She placed her lips on the edge and sipped a little. "Mmm, it's sweet," she cooed.

"I put a little honey in it."

"What time is it?" She glanced around. The bright sunny view she had fallen asleep to earlier had darkened.

"Almost dinnertime." He set the cup on the bedside table. "I hate to say it—"

"I know. Rekkus will have a conniption if we aren't on time for dinner." She stretched her neck from side to side.

"How's our princess?" Arawn strolled to the other side of the bed and plopped down beside her.

"Much better, thanks." She smoothed her hair back with relief. "I can't believe what a pain in the rump I've been. I spoiled your whole week with this nonsense."

"Are you kidding us?" Kane chuckled. "We've been skinny dipping, seen you cut loose, and best of all, we got out of getting our asses kicked by Rekkus ten hours a day."

"You got that right, brother!" Arawn held a fist across for Kane to knuckle bump with him. "Training is brutal. We're much happier here with you." He winked.

Trinity studied his luscious lips curved into a fantastic smile. With an angular jaw and the black ink peeking out of the sleeves and collar of his shirt, his jet-black hair and deep, dark eyes, Arawn was stunning. She glanced to find Kane's adoring gaze light up his incredible green eyes. These men were spectacular, protective, and devoted to her, at least for the week.

"I want to ask you both something, and please"— she glanced between them—"be honest with me."

"Of course," they replied in unison.

She sucked in a long, shaky breath. "Did I do or say anything I should be terribly embarrassed about last night at dinner, or after?"

"You don't remember." Kane's smile faded. "You were a delight."

"Really?" She glared at him in disbelief.

"Truthfully, you were less uptight, overall. You were fine. There's nothing to worry about."

"What did I talk about?" She had been heavily sedated with herbs and worried her blabbermouth ways had gotten the best of her, which was why she didn't drink in the mundane world often.

"Not much." Kane fixed his gaze on the cup of tea.

"You promised to be honest with me," she grumbled.

"Look, you may have mentioned a little about your parents and your uncle," Arawn confessed. "But it wasn't bad at all."

"Oh." She slouched her shoulders.

"You did mention a few things about us that took me by surprise." Arawn folded his arms across his rippling chest. His biceps bulged.

"Such as?"

"You told Kane here you saw stone and wings."

"Arawn," Kane growled and bared his teeth.

"Don't sweat it, buddy." He shook his head. "I think it's okay." He waited while she searched her brain for any recollection.

"That's right. And a heart of stone?"

"Yeah, and with me?" he prompted.

"Hmm...." She squinted hard as she thought. "Oh,

yes. She opened her eyes and stared at him. You're conflicted with your good nature, war, and revenge...and hounds with red ears?"

"How do you see those things?" Kane's voice became a soft murmur. "Are you clairvoyant?" He tucked his chin to his chest and avoided eye contact.

"Not exactly, but I get flashes of thoughts sometimes. My talents have been way off-kilter for months. Now, I can't turn it on when I want, or more so recently, shut it off." She paused and reflected on the pieces she did recall. "What did those things mean?"

"The stone and wings?" Kane shrugged.

"Or the conflict and war?" Arawn held his palms up with confusion.

"All of it?"

The two friends gawked at one another for a long moment. Frustration festered deep inside her. "Hey," she snapped. "I poured out my guts to you two last night, and not of my volition. Things I've never told another living soul. You owe me the truth. Now spill it, both of you."

"It should be pretty easy to figure out." Kane pursed his lips. "Heart of stone, wings, total carnivore and I guard at night on top of the roof...."

The pieces slipped together in perfect harmony. "You're a gargoyle?"

"I am." He grimaced and turned his head to the side.

"Look at me, Kane?" She cupped his chin and prompted him to meet her gaze. His eyes held the darkness of profound shame. "You're wonderful."

"You don't think gargoyles are grotesque?" His surprise stunned her.

"I'd never met one in person before now. How could I find someone who's stuck by my side to protect me grotesque?"

"Maybe not in this form." He grasped her hand and removed it from his chin.

"If you doubt me, then show me and I'll prove you wrong."

"You want me to change into a gargoyle?" He choked.

"Yes."

"No...." He shook his head. "Never in front of you."

"Why not?"

"Because, it would scare you, and I don't ever want you to be scared of me, I couldn't bear it."

Arawn cleared his throat. "Once, a long time ago, a woman he saved screamed bloody murder and ran away from him. She called him a demon."

Kane snarled at Arawn. "Traitor."

"She needs to know why it's such an issue. Seemed like a pretty good time since we've shared all our secrets." He shrugged.

"Someone you saved reacted in fear...let me guess, a mundane?" Trinity needed to dissect this deep-seated indignity he tried to avoid.

"She was." He dipped his chin.

"Humans are raised with fairytales and fables of us all." She pointed to her white locks and motioned to her pale features and bright blue eyes. "They view us as monsters, not because it's true, but due to the limitations of knowledge they have. I don't imagine many mundanes would react any differently."

"No, I would guess not," he concurred.

"But"—she inched a little closer and set her fingers under his chin again to meet her gaze—"for the record, you are a very handsome guy." The apex between her thighs warmed with her confession.

Kane picked up her hand and kissed the back of her knuckles. "You're pretty damn amazing yourself."

"Your turn." She leered at Arawn. "Conflicted, kind, but war torn and revenge driven?"

"Your friendly neighborhood Lord of the Underworld at your service, ma'am." He flashed a forced grin. "Or at least, I'm next in line for the throne."

"Arawn?" The name sounded vaguely familiar, but couldn't place it. Her time in the mundane world had dulled her knowledge of para history.

"Junior. My father is the original Arawn of Annwn."

"You're immortal?"

"I am." He rubbed his thighs and avoided her gaze.

"Why are you here?" She frowned.

"I...abdicated my claim to the throne." He rolled his shoulders.

"Go on, the rest of it?" she demanded. "What are you hiding behind those tattoos? Let me see."

Arawn grimaced. "I don't...take my shirt off."

"Now."

Arawn pulled the edges of his black T-shirt out of the waist of his pants and inched it up his muscular torso and over his head. Trinity finally got her close-up and undistorted view of the tribal tattoos adorning his body from waist to neck and across his biceps. Black ink decorated this decadent canvas of muscle. She traced her fingers over the design from his collar down to the front of his chest. The pads of her fingers grazed over a raised, rough patch of skin. The tattoos camouflaged a jagged nine-or-so inch scar from his sternum to his shoulder.

"What happened to you?"

Arawn pressed his lips tight.

"He freed me from his father's prison, along with many other souls. Arawn senior had a bit of a temper. He liked to sic his hounds of hell on those who defied him. It's now referred to as the Battle of Annwn."

"Because?"

"My buddy here rose up against his father, who stood for war, revenge. He had enslaved the souls of the damned as his personal dog pack."

"How terrible!" A ripple of devastation shuddered through her chest.

"Arawn saved my life. He gave me my freedom, and, for that, I'm forever indebted to him." Kane reached over and patted his friend on the shoulder. "But the goofball kind of grows on you after a while, too."

"You both do, you big lugs." Trinity took their hands and held onto them. "So it would seem I'm not the only one with a dark past."

"No, pretty lady, you most certainly are not." Arawn's features lightened a little with his smile.

Trinity shuddered. "Your father?" She ran her fingertips over the raised skin again. "I'm so sorry."

"Yeah, he's kind of a prick." Arawn shrugged.

"I'd say so." She caressed his arm. He sat hunched forward.

"I noticed, Kane, you have some impressive artwork yourself." This up close and personal became far more than she intended, on a dangerous level, but she couldn't help herself. She wanted to see more.

"I do." Kane lifted his T-shirt to reveal a detailed symbol on his chest of exquisite dark wings circled around writing she didn't recognize.

"What does it say?"

"It's Gaelic for protector of the innocent."

"Beautiful." Upon further inspection, she found Celtic knot work mixed with tribal strokes of black ink banded around his biceps. "You had more on your back, didn't you?"

"Yes." He shifted sideways. On his spectacular

canvas of taut skin wrapped over bulging muscles, he bared the tribal artwork of a Celtic cross and wings surrounding it.

"It's incredible."

"Well, I couldn't let pretty boy over there outdo me in catching the ladies' attention with all his fancy ink."

"Joke all you want, but it's meaningful and exquisite." Fascinated, she skated her palm over the details. "Both of you." Trinity folded her hands and rested them in her lap. "I have to admit, on first impression, I thought you were both sailors here to get laid. I had no idea how honorable and strong you both are."

"Are you getting all mushy on us?" Kane slipped his shirt back over his head and threaded his arms through the sleeves.

Arawn did the same, and disappointment filled her. What she wouldn't give to know how they felt about her right now. Were they as turned on as she was? If so, it could promise a week to remember.

The realization struck her like a bolt of lightning. "I can see your expression, but I can't feel your thoughts right now."

"It's the necklace the sisters made for you." Arawn lifted the heavy stone and metal from her chest. "A talisman to protect you from getting overpowered by your abilities. They got it ready while you slept."

"It's beautiful. This fixes everything?" She cupped her hand over his.

He shook his head. "It's only temporary, I'm afraid."

"I don't understand. I can't read your thoughts or feel anything right now." She let go of his hand, and he released the necklace.

"We aren't sure what's happened to you, but the

Rowans suspect it's an attack against you."

Her chest constricted. "For what? I haven't done anything wrong."

"We know, but we have to figure out why someone stole pieces of your memory." Kane rubbed her thigh with a swirl of his fingertips.

"Is there a time limit on its power?"

"I don't think it's that type of temporary." Kane tilted his head. "Part of the test will be dinnertime...if you can handle it?"

"How will dinner test this necklace?"

"Right now, there are only us three here." Arawn lifted her hand and placed a kiss on the inside of her wrist, which made butterflies dance in her tummy. "They want to see how you cope around other energies, paras, and humans, in the dinner hall. Then we will take it from there."

The dancing butterflies bottomed out at the thought of the extreme pain she'd suffered earlier in the day. "I don't think I can—"

"We'll be right there with you. We won't let anything happen." Arawn cradled her cheek in the heat of his palm. "If you start to feel, we leave, right then and there."

"Okay." Her inner strength resurfaced with the touch of his skin to hers.

"We've got you." Kane tucked a stray strand of hair behind her ear.

His words resonated through her body like an aphrodisiac.

Oh, I hope so. Both of you.

A shimmer of excitement curled around her spine at the thought of having them all to herself. Trinity cleared her throat and inched back a little. She still couldn't read them, or how they could possibly feel about her. They'd shared their tales, and they were devoted to protecting her. But aside from a few kind words and a gentle affection, they'd offered no concrete indicators they wanted her as much as she wanted them.

"I'd better freshen up."

Chapter Eight

T rinity dreaded her pending arrival to the dinner hall. The mere thought of the pain she had endured earlier sent her anxieties through the roof. Trinity gripped the cool talisman in her palm and drew in slow breaths, desperate not to feel anything, except maybe relief.

She had not been prepared to have the companionship of two sexy men, let alone be so completely taken by them. The reason for her trip to the island had been to work through her grief, but this became a temporary distraction promising to result in heartache. After all, they were assigned to her for protection. Once the week passed and she returned to New York, what would happen then? She'd be all alone, and likely further attacked by whatever forces meant her harm.

What could she have possibly done to warrant an attack of any sort? She made her entire existence about helping others in pain, not producing it. Could it have to do with the pieces of her memory that had mysteriously disappeared, especially the death of her uncle. She'd been there. Did some entity blame her for his death? Or had she in some way been responsible for the vile torture he endured before he died?

"Hey, you okay?" Kane, on her left side, rubbed her back as they strolled into the Haus.

"Sure."

"Just say the word, and we'll take dinner to go." Arawn brushed the back of his knuckles against her cheek. "We're right here with you."

She drew in a deep inhale, and the savory aroma of roast chicken filled her nostrils. Her stomach gave a vicious grumble, and she gripped it with embarrassment. "I am pretty hungry," she confessed.

"So we hear." Arawn smirked.

"Hopefully, Sage will let you have more than salad tonight." Kane rubbed her shoulder.

"That would be nice."

Arawn held out a chair for her at the quaint circular table, and she sat down. He and Kane took their seats across from her. Facing the eye candy made it difficult to hold onto the mental decision to stay focused on the treatments the Rowans offered her this week and nothing more.

Minimal eye contact, she coached herself. *Don't look at their captivating eyes, their succulent lips, or broad shoulders. Don't stare at their bulging biceps or rock-solid chests, and, whatever you do, Trinity, do* not *glance below the waist. You can't handle the curiosity right now.*

Thirst countered her hormonal distress. She licked her parched lips, picked up her wine glass filled with ice water, and downed half of it.

"I know that look." Arawn cracked a one-sided grin.

She choked mid-sip. "Excuse me?"

"You're starving." He patted her hand.

Trinity's core rippled with longing under his penetrating gaze and his simple touch. "You have no idea."

A half chicken, a plate full of salad, potatoes, and sautéed vegetables later, she began to feel more like her old self.

"Wow, I had no idea you had such an appetite." Arawn gawped at her empty plate with amusement.

"Hope you don't mind. I'm not much of a dainty girl when it comes to food." Although she was a voluptuous para, she was grateful her curves were in all the right places, and she loved her food. Finished with her meal, she contemplated chocolate-anything to gratify her sweet tooth. At least these cravings she had the means to satiate, unlike her sexual starvation.

"Not in the least." Kane wiped his mouth and discarded his napkin onto the table. "It's a relief to see a beautiful woman not afraid to enjoy a good meal."

Surprise cascaded over her with his kind words. "You think I'm beautiful?"

"Uh, yeah, we established that last night when you scolded me for my...immoral thoughts." Kane flashed a roguish grin.

"I did?" She glanced between him and Arawn and rubbed her temples with irritation. "You must think I'm a complete basket case."

"No, we don't." Arawn spoke in a deep, velvety tone. "And in case you don't recall this either, I think you're pretty damn sexy, too."

"Oh." Her cheeks flooded with heat. *Did he really call me sexy? Thank the gods. I may actually have a chance with these incredible men. Did we discuss this last night?* Trinity tried to recall their comments. "Maybe there is a hint of...." She fixed her gaze on her water glass. What did she remember? Their swim in the hot springs, but she couldn't read anything there.

Last night was a blank page. Then, one memory rushed back—their first encounter. "My spectacular entrance through the portal," she announced with triumph. "That, I remember."

"What exactly do you recall?" Arawn popped his eyes wide with amusement.

"I remember I crash landed on you!" She pointed at him. "I felt so clumsy and embarrassed. And I tried to sit up." Her core fluttered as the images settled in her mind of how she sat on top of the tall, dark, exotic man.

"When you pinned me to the floor?" He chuckled.

"I accidentally straddled you, after I tackled you."

Arawn dropped his napkin in his lap. "I didn't mind in the least." His gaze held an appetite she recognized.

Unease settled over her body. "I find you both extremely attractive, too, but—"

"Pardon us for interrupting your cozy dinner." A sultry voice broke through their heated topic.

Trinity glanced to her side to find three familiar women skulking toward them. They circled their table, their ample cleavage spilling over each of their too-small, ebony ribbed corsets. Dressed similarly—the only difference the colored trim of their bodices, one dark purple, one crimson, and one gold—their curly locks of blonde, red, and brunette cascaded over their shoulders. They were three versions of a female rival's basic nightmare—exquisite. Draped with flimsy black miniskirts and adorned with Gothic styled lace bracelets on their right hands and black beaded chains attached to rings on their index fingers, these women screamed horny bitches with an agenda.

"What do you want?" Trinity seethed.

"We couldn't help but overhear your conversation

as we passed by," the redhead purred in a seductive tone. "If you're not into these fine specimens, we're happy to...take care of their primal needs." She narrowed her eyes, and her lips curled into a sadistic grin.

Searing red filled Trinity's vision, and she jumped up. "It's rude to eavesdrop, and it's even more offensive to crush on someone else's escorts," she spat with hatred.

"But these two"—the blonde behind Arawn hummed and caressed his shoulders—"are so handsome and virile. You shouldn't be greedy, sweetheart."

Arawn remained still, dazed, as the object of Trinity's irritation groped his muscular arms. She chewed the inside of her lip while tremors of rage rolled over her body.

The brunette paused at Kane's side and ran her long fingers through his auburn mane. He held the identical blank stare his immortal friend wore. "My sister is right," the brunette blathered. "We're here to work out our grief, and these rugged men could easily distract us from bereaving the tragic deaths of our parents. It was a murder-suicide, you know. Horrific," she tsked. "We can't work past the ghastly images burned into our memories.... Do you know what I mean?"

"Maybe you should seek therapy," Trinity sneered.

Fraught with the desperate need to rip the women's hair from their scalps and gouge their eyes out, she froze on the spot, powerless to respond further. She stared helplessly as her tormentor trailed her fingers over her cleavage and leaned in to whisper to Arawn. Trinity spied the ring on her right hand, a symbol of a red serpent's eye framed in a triangle of three lightning bolts.

With her glasses on, she couldn't see their auras, but would bet her life they were each cloaked in a veil of dark evil. Other than the slutty overstepping and their obvious interest in robbing her of her escorts, Trinity couldn't read their thoughts either. Frustration mounted. She reached to pull her protective talisman off, frantic to decipher their intentions.... *By the gods, I can't move!*

Trinity ached to scream profanities at their intrusion. Her lips had numbed, and she found it impossible to force the words out of her mouth. She was helpless even to storm away.

One of the harlot's black eyes morphed into the same blood-red serpent eyes from her ring. The other two twisted toward Trinity, glaring with the same terrifying red orbs.

Her eyelids grew heavy, and she fought to keep them open. A magnetic pull drew her focus from her tormentors. The bright lights overhead blared, and she squinted to block it out.

"But you don't want to hook up with two guys?" Kane's voice faded.

"W-what?" she muttered. The air grew thick around her. Her chest constricted, and she struggled to breathe.

A firm grip on her wrist jolted her. "Princess?"

She shook her head, surprised to find Arawn and Kane both stood in front of her with wide eyes. "What?"

"Where were you going?" Kane crooked his head and blocked her line of vision. "Hey, are you with us?"

The haze around her vision started to lift. She glanced around. "Where did they go?"

"Who?" Kane cupped her cheek.

"The three women." She swallowed hard.

"What women, darlin'?" Kane gripped her shoulders, his voice low and stern.

"Those." She spun around as she tried to locate the trio of seduction. "They were just here!"

"There is no one but us," Arawn told her. "There are other guests dining here, but no one has approached us. We were talking, and you went quiet and stood to leave."

"But they hit on you both. I couldn't move or speak." Tears pricked her eyes. "Tell me you saw them."

"We need to get you to the siblings, now." Arawn took her by the hand. "Can you walk?"

"Yes."

The immortal headed out the dining hall door, his strides so long and fast she had to jog to keep pace with him. Kane followed.

What the hell happened? How could everything come crashing down so hard in a matter of minutes?

Have I really lost my mind?

Chapter Nine

In the Rowans' office, Trinity took a seat in the wooden chair and shivered. Kane sat beside her and held her close with one arm.

"Tell me what you saw." Sage soothed in a soft voice. "Did you feel anything?"

"I couldn't read their thoughts, just what they said out loud."

Cemil entered the room with Cyrus, and Rekkus and Myron followed them in. "Trinity, bear with me, but I need Myron to read for you."

She hesitated and glanced up to Arawn.

"It's okay. She can see things in her cards. It might help."

Kane removed his arm from her shoulder and Myron sat down across the desk from her. The redhead shuffled her deck and began to lay the cards in what seemed to be a random order.

"These are my baba's cards." Myron flipped them over one at a time. "Oh, my."

"What do you see?" Trinity gawked at the cards in terror.

"See here, this is a one-eyed royal, the king of diamonds. Beside him is the queen of diamonds, and here, is the three of diamonds."

"Okay?" Trinity shrugged.

"On top is the three of hearts. That's you." Myron cocked her head to the side, her eyes widening. "I see the evil eye. That's the king." She pointed to the card in question. "I'm not clear why the queen is here. Perhaps a spouse? And the three of diamonds. I see three women on the attack."

Trinity glared at the shape the cards had been placed in, and a wave of ice-cold shock rolled over her skin. "A lightning bolt?"

"Yes, it would seem so." Myron agreed.

"I remember...." She glanced around the desk. "I need a paper and something to draw with."

Myron tugged open the drawer and handed her a blank piece of paper and a pencil. Trinity closed her eyes to better see the image flashing across her mind. She drew in crude strokes. After a few minutes, she set the pencil down.

"This is what I remember. Three lightning bolts in the shape of a triangle with a red serpent's eye in the center."

"You two didn't see anyone?" Cyrus stared at Arawn and Kane.

"No," Arawn concurred. "We just ate dinner. She seemed fine. We talked, and then she went blank and got up to leave."

Myron placed the remainder of her deck down. "Trinity, you didn't imagine this. There were three women there, tormenting you."

"Who?" Rekkus stepped closer.

"It would appear to be the three sisters in question." Myron nodded. "The blonde, brunette, and redhead. They're the three of diamonds."

"How could they get to her? We were right there." Kane put his arm around her again as she trembled. The warmth and tenderness of his touch was only topped by the safety and strength she cherished, nestled under his muscular arm.

"My guess would be the same way they managed to get to her last night and cause the severe headache," Cyrus remarked. "And put Kane in a trance of some sort."

"The talisman worked a little tonight, but not enough," Cemil muttered. "You couldn't read anyone's thoughts, you're not in pain and didn't get overwhelmed with other's baggage. But they attacked you on a subconscious level." He pursed his lips. "I'd guarantee they're the ones messing with your memory, too. Since you could remember this symbol, maybe they don't have the same control they did before."

White-hot anger flooded her chest at the serpent eye framed by three lightning bolts. "I can see it as clear as day. They each had black lace bracelets with chains to rings on their index fingers with this symbol." She tapped her finger on the paper. "The serpent's eye was red." She forced a swallow past the lump in her throat. "Then their black eyes changed to the same as the ring."

"What?" Arawn moved to the edge of the desk and studied her drawing, his handsome features now marred with distress.

"Do you know who they are?" Rekkus interjected.

"I have an idea." He scrubbed his face. "When my father wanted to dole out punishment for any sins brought to his attention, he would appoint the Three Furies to exact justice on the intended targets."

"The Furies?" Kane's grip on her shoulder tightened. The intensity of his touch matched the panic coursing through her veins.

"Yes. And that symbol, the red eye?" Arawn pointed to the sketch.

"What about it?" Trinity stared at the offensive image.

"It's the Evil Eye. Used as a tool to dish out some of the punishment."

"How?" Sage inched forward to sit on the edge of her chair. "My knowledge is of the light arts. Darker elements I tend to learn on a need-to-know basis."

Arawn gritted his teeth. "The Furies are the goddesses of vengeance and retribution."

"I've heard of them, but don't know anything about them. I thought they were around centuries ago." Trinity's throat grew thick as the threat became clearer, every muscle in her body wracked with tension.

"They are the daughters of Nyx, the Ancient Dark Goddess. Usually, they're horrible winged women, draped in black, with serpent hair and eyes dripping blood. It would seem their agenda isn't all they've managed to cloak. They changed their appearances, too."

"Tears of blood?" The familiar words settled in Trinity's stomach like cement.

"Not tears, princess. Vengeance." The tenor of defeat tinged Arawn's words. "The Furies epitomize conscience and punish crimes. The Dread Ones have the ability to drive their victims insane, hence the Latin name *Furor*. They have the power to erase your memory and leave the trauma to afflict you."

"By the Gods...." She could barely force a whisper past the lump in her throat. A plethora of emotions flooded her weary brain. Beyond the white-hot shock that settled into her bones, a tidal wave of terror had managed to take the lead, and a swell of rage had slipped into a close second.

"These sisters who checked in; does anyone know their names?" Sage glanced around the room.

"They registered as Megan, Tish, and Alex Erines," Rekkus spoke up.

"That confirms it, then." Arawn exhaled a heavy sigh. "They're also known as Erinyes in Greek Mythology. Their names are Megaera, Tisiphone, and Alecto."

"I did attendance at the dining hall. Those three were there at the beginning of dinner." Rekkus growled. "I sent security to the rooms and they weren't there. We haven't been able to locate them since."

As she absorbed the avalanche of information, rage spiked up Trinity's spine. "You said they exact punishment and vengeance?"

"Yeah." Arawn agreed. Still at the edge of the desk, he shifted his weight and folded his arms across his chest, now in a defensive stance. He was just as worried as she was, by the looks of him, maybe even more.

"They're basically hired guns?" she persisted. *Who would send these creatures after me? What in Tartarus could I have done to warrant this attack?* Pins and needles prickled her fingertips. She glanced down to her clenched fists. Her knuckles had whitened.

"They are."

"I haven't done anything wrong. Why me?" she demanded. *I've lost my entire family, and these sadistic creatures are driving me mad? For what purpose?*

"I'm not sure, but we'll figure it out." Arawn maneuvered behind Trinity and caressed her shoulders. "Sometimes, they're vigilant about crimes that were committed within a family, murders of parents are considered as the most heinous of crimes. I've heard tales of when they would haunt a son who had failed to avenge a parent who had been killed unjustly. The Furies are ruthless. They would hound their victim until the person makes reckoning on the death of their parents...or...."

Trinity twisted around and glared at Arawn. "Or?"

"They would die somehow, either by their hand, or by that of an innocent they drove insane to do their bidding." The depth of his gray eyes framed by his ebony lashes had now darkened to black as coal. His luscious lips were pressed tight. Stress and worry clouded the magnificence of his features.

"So you think I'm haunted by these Bitches of Eastwick because I haven't avenged the murder of my parents?"

"No, but we can't rule it out. Your parents were murdered, and now they're after you."

"I saw it. It was a murder-suicide," Cyrus disputed in a slow, deliberate voice.

Trinity turned back to find the stern glare Cyrus flashed. She recognized the pain his gaze held. The images he referred to about their deaths troubled him as much now, as they had earlier.

"What you saw, and what may really have happened may not be one in the same." Arawn lowered his voice and squeezed her shoulders. "They possess the power to alter perception and memory as we've witnessed here. We need to get more information to better understand this."

"Fair enough. Now that we know who they are and that they were sent, we have to figure out why and by whom." The distress that filled Cyrus' face settled in her gut like a rock.

"I'm very familiar with the Evil Eye," Sarka piped up from her chair in the corner beside Sage. "But never with a triangle of lightning bolts."

"Yeah," Arawn grumbled. "That's a problem, too."

"Why?" Sarka prompted him to continue.

"In the ancient world, a lightning bolt is a symbol for supernatural power used by the male gods."

"What does it mean?" Trinity rested her head against Kane's solid chest.

"It means there is a powerful alliance at work here. The triangular Evil Eye is an ancient symbol of power in the hierarchy of the Underworld."

"Could it have anything to do with my uncle's death?" *Maybe it is my fault....*

"I highly doubt it." Arawn moved back to the desk and faced her, his frown sending shivers down her spine. "This symbol is associated with superior leadership. One mortal death wouldn't warrant this kind of retribution on a para in my experience. This is something much deeper."

"Is the sovereign of the banshee considered a high power?" she persisted. *Surely there is some way to stop them. Find out who sent them and go straight to the source? Or perhaps I can run and hide? My uncle had me do it for decades, so why not now?*

"Not in the Underworld, but I wouldn't rule out a possible connection." Arawn stroked her hair. His touch carried a bitter sweetness.

"There is no way to get information from the Underworld about this, is there?" Rekkus asked.

"We both burned that bridge a long time ago, I'm afraid." Arawn replied in a soft tone. "I may be able to call in a favor or two. I'll need some time to contact some old acquaintances."

"We don't appear to have much time." Rekkus said. "Do what you can. In the meanwhile, you two continue to protect her twenty-four hours a day."

"Understood," Kane agreed.

"Tomorrow," Cemil softened his serious voice, "you and I, Trinity, have some work to do in the

Elysian Fields. Perhaps we can gain some insight on a different plane of existence."

"Okay." She settled into Kane's embrace.

"For tonight, another session with Serena in the hot springs," Cemil volunteered. "And a good night's sleep. It's critical you unwind as much as possible. You'll need all your strength for tomorrow."

"What about security?" Sarka inquired.

"Since they can affect her without anyone else seeing them, there isn't much more we can do." Rekkus growled.

"I think we may have a bit of a break for now." Arawn offered.

Cyrus cocked his head. "How so?"

"A few things, first, the Evil Eye explains the plumbing, heating, and cooling issues on the second floor. It can also cause the nausea the para guests have complained of."

"Even though they are clearly after Trinity," Kane interceded, "we can gauge their hidden presence by these symptoms. It's a natural side effect of the Evil Eye. If you can post ample para security around the cabin, keep everyone on radio check-in, we can possibly pick up on their proximity to her. We may not see them, but the nausea is a telltale sign they're close."

"In my experience with the Furies," Arawn continued, "once they've made their presence known to the victim, it will be a little while before they try to strike the final blow. In part, because they let their victims stew, drive themselves crazy with worry. The Furies are plotting now, and the security and talisman the sisters made for Trinity have alerted them we know they're here."

"Will they physically attack her?" Kane asked the question burning in Trinity's mind.

"No, of that I'm certain." Arawn's words brought little comfort. "They drive their victims mad, but don't exact physical violence. They do possess the ability to provoke others to it, so we have to be careful who is around Trinity until this is resolved."

"Is there some sort of magical assist we can provide the rest of us with so we aren't affected by them?" Sarka asked.

"I wouldn't do it for the extra security." Arawn's voice was deep and stern. "We need them untainted so they can physically sense their presence. However, if there is any way to whip up enchanted amulets for us all here who are aware of what's going on, Nazar Boncugu will counter the Furies' powers."

Sarka scrunched her nose. "What is a Nazar Boncugu?"

"It's the Evil Eye Bead. It can deflect the harm they project from their symbols."

"It has to be constructed of blue glass of Antolia," Arawn instructed. "You may want to fashion it framed with a Wiccan symbol of power."

"A triquetra," Sarka agreed. "I have design in mind."

"We need one for each of us." Arawn circled his hand in the air, indicating everyone in the room. "We will keep Trinity away from the rest of the Wiccan Haus guests and staff for now."

Sage stood to join her sister. "Do we have blue glass of Antolia?"

"We do." Sarka headed out the door with Sage in pursuit.

Chapter Ten

B ack at the villa on the water, Trinity found herself more relaxed than she thought possible, given the circumstances. The dip in the springs with Serena soothed her aching muscles and eased some of her tension, although it was a temporary fix.

"I don't see all the extra security." She stood on the porch and scouted the edges of the water.

"They're hidden out of view, but there are nine security guys posted all around us." Kane caressed the small of her back. "We've got you covered, darlin'."

"I know you do." She trembled as icy chills encased her skin. "I still don't understand. Why me?"

"Cemil hopes your trip to the Elysian Fields will reveal more information." Arawn opened the door. "In the meantime, everyone is armed with the amulets Sarka and Sage put together." He held up the silver triquetra with the blue glass and a detailed cobalt eye in the center.

"Wow, they are good, and fast." Trinity admired the crafted glasswork.

Once the trio ventured inside the villa, Kane locked the door and set a square black device on the coffee table. The tiny red light beamed.

"What's that for?" She pointed to the black device.

"It's a walkie-talkie. The security team and the Rowans all have them set to the same frequency. As long as there's even the slightest concern the Furies are around, we all need to stay in close communication." Arawn tucked his arm around her shoulder. "It's all good. You'll get the rest you need tonight."

"Now we're held hostage in this cabin, you'll both be bored out of your minds," she lamented. "All because of me."

"It's not so tragic to hang out with you." Kane brushed back a loose strand of hair and tucked it behind her ear. Butterflies danced in her belly under his touch, but her throat remained thick with fright.

"I've got a few things in mind to pass the time." Arawn winked with a playful grin.

"Oh really?" She backed away. "I'm not sure I want to know...." So much of her hoped they wanted to spend the night under the covers with her, but deep-seated fears crashed back to the surface. *Don't get close, everyone you care for dies a horrible death. Spare their lives and keep some distance, for the love of Hades, don't be selfish.*

"You don't trust us, Trinity?" Arawn stepped closer, and she backed up farther until she bumped against the wall by the bedroom.

"Uh, of course I do...it's just..."

Arawn braced his palm against the wall beside her shoulder and leaned toward her, his face dangerously close to hers. His heat intoxicated her as she sucked in a shuddering inhale. "I've got a little fun planned for us three."

The sweet warmth of his breath brushed over her face. "What...do, uh...you have in mind?" she stammered.

He gripped the handle beside her and tugged the door next to her open. "I kind of enjoyed how you cut loose the other night." He reached into the linen closet. "There has been far too much stress on your shoulders these past few days."

"Agreed," she whispered, her gaze fixed on his.

Was he reaching for silk sheets? Damn if she hadn't wished away her ability to read his thoughts. Right now, she had no clue what he plotted.

"How about a little fun with us?" He pulled something out of the closet, slowly inched away from her, and set a long, thin box into her shaky hands.

She gazed up into the depths of his darkly seductive eyes and bit her bottom lip.

"I'll make some space." He headed back to the living room and got Kane to help him move the furniture against the walls.

Trinity swallowed hard. Her cheeks warmed, and her core thrummed with need. She glanced down at the box and blinked in surprise. "Twister?"

"Why not?" Kane high-fived his comrade. "Great idea."

"You're kidding, right?" *A child's game, while you've got me all hot and bothered? What's next, coloring with crayons?*

"What's the problem?" Arawn returned to her and collected the box from her grasp. "I found this in the Game Shack."

"What are we, ten years old?" *There is absolutely nothing I associate as fun with this ludicrous idea. What is it?* She lifted the lid and inspected the folded plastic material and the cardboard spinner. *Real rocket science here.*

"You're worried it won't be enough of a challenge for us grown-ups?" he taunted. "We can make it more interesting, if you like."

"How?" Skeptical he would have a reasonable answer, she stood still and waited for the juicy details. *Strip Twister with the two hot paras? I might not be able to resist.*

"Don't tell Rekkus, but I snuck in a little contraband this week." He handed the game to Kane. "Set it up. I'll be right back."

Arawn strolled toward her again and palmed her cheek and flashed a teasing smirk. He went back into the closet, dragged out a hefty duffle bag, and fished through it. "Here we go," he announced and pulled out a large glass bottle and dropped the bag back on the floor.

"What have you got?" Kane spread the multi-colored plastic mat across the bamboo floor.

"My old friend, ouzo."

"Ouzo?" Trinity studied the bottle. The label was written in Greek, therefore, indecipherable to her.

"It's a drink that tastes like Anise and black licorice. It's sweet, intense, and a little dangerous." He cupped her chin and kissed her forehead. "Just like you, princess."

Although she wouldn't admit it to them, the prospect of upping the stakes intrigued Trinity. Even as a small kid, she never played games or had fun of any kind. Her childhood had been a blur of trauma and seclusion. Her uncle hid her away and shielded her as much as he could until she became an obstinate adult and insisted they move to New York and live a mundane existence. By then, in college and straight forward into a career, she perfected the existence of all work and no fun. Board games were not a para-norm, but she knew a little about Twister. She'd seen commercials about the precarious positions people could contort themselves into in a ploy to be the last player standing, or rather crouching.

"So, what's the ouzo for?"

"Makes it more adult." Arawn headed to the kitchen and searched through the cupboards. He returned with three glass tumblers in hand. "Consider it a little fun, a test of your agility and a chance to stop thinking so much."

"Fine," she mocked. "But you both have an advantage with me in a sundress." She rushed to her suitcase and riffled through her clothes. "If I play, it's gonna be to win." She tugged out a white tank top and a pair of black yoga pants. "Excuse me, gentlemen." Trinity slipped into the bathroom and suited up.

Arawn poured three shots of ouzo.

"Okay, let's get this party started." Trinity returned to the living room.

Arawn pressed his lips tight, a little disappointed she'd changed out of her revealing sundress, he nonetheless studied the way her tank top hugged her voluptuous curves, as did her yoga pants. Although she still wore her hair pinned up in a tight bun, she remained a vision of divine temptation. He admired her pretty bare toes, nails painted a glossy red, and grinned.

"What's so funny?" She accepted the glass he handed her.

"Nothing, I thought perhaps your attire would be less distracting than your sundress." He glanced down at her creamy mounds peeking above the low neckline of her top. "But I was wrong." He gulped hard. "Is there anything you don't look good in?"

"Glad I wasn't the only one who thought so." Kane

clinked glasses with him.

"Down boys." Trinity tossed back her shot.

Arawn studied her face and waited for a shudder or some other reaction of shock at the strong taste. Instead, she swallowed, licked her ruby lips, and held the glass out for a second shot.

"It's tasty."

Arawn sputtered. "I think we have a ringer here. We may be in over our heads." He poured her another shot and sucked back his own. Kane did the same.

She removed her rose-colored glasses and set them on the table beside the bottle of booze.

"What are you doing?" Arawn stared in disbelief at her bright blue eyes.

"Your auras don't upset me, and this game might get...awkward. I'd hate to break them by accident."

"Fair enough." He poured her another shot. It was a pleasant development to see her comfort level advance. He had longed to stare into the depths of her cerulean-blue eyes without the hindrance of the pink lenses.

"Okay, you big lugs, tell me the rules so I can kick both your asses." She sucked back her second shot, set the glass on the table, and stood at the edge of the mat. "Second round and neither of you can keep up?" She eyed their empty glasses. "It's gonna be a short night."

Arawn chuckled and topped up both drinks. He and Kane chugged theirs and joined her at the mat.

"We take turns and spin the wheel. Whatever color, side, and limb it tells you, you have to move, left hand, red, right foot, blue..." Kane explained.

"Got it." She nodded. "Let's begin."

She glowed with excitement. He hadn't expected this to go over half as well as it had. He'd convinced himself he'd have to bribe her to even start the game.

Six moves each into the game, and they had all played it safe till now, all in their neat little corners of blended moves.

"Is this all there is to this?" Trinity tsked.

"A few more moves, and it will get tricky, I assure you," Kane warned her.

"Sure it will. There is no challenge here."

"Hold that thought." Arawn took note of his placement and jumped up from the mat. He poured three more shots and brought them to his opponents. He held the glass to her luscious lips, and she tried to reach to grab it.

"Uh, uh, uh." He pulled back. "Players have to keep in position."

"Then why are you up?"

"I'm the bartender." He held the glass again. "Go on. I won't spill it. Trust me."

"Never trust a man who says trust me." She glared at him, but he tipped the contents into her mouth.

"What's that supposed to mean?" Kane exhaled, hunched over.

"My mother used to tell me, never trust a man who says trust me." She snickered.

"Well, I don't mean to speak ill of her, but, did I spill it?" He wished he had the nerve to spill it.

"Not yet, but there's still plenty of time...and ouzo." She winked.

Arawn's balls tightened at the innuendo. *There may be hope for this adventure yet.*

Was this the start of her shift into the brazen woman they'd witnessed after Sage's herbal roofie? Did enticing her with alcohol make him a deviant? He didn't want to think so, but guilt permeated his brain nonetheless. After all, the Lord of the Underworld had a knack for getting what he wanted with little regard for right or wrong. Or, at least, that was how he'd rolled in his younger days.

Service in the Para Elite Forces was cut and dry with no blurred lines to navigate. Unlike now, with Trinity. He wanted her, more than any woman he'd ever set eyes on. But they'd been assigned to protect her, not seduce her. Was his playful ploy to get close to her putting her at risk of harm? His desire for her awakened the dark nature he had worked so hard to suppress. The closer he got to her, the more blurred his lines grew, and the less he cared about right or wrong.

"What about mine?" Kane grunted and tried to reach the second glass with his mouth.

"Oh, yeah." He held the cup for his buddy to chug.

Arawn worked to push his self-doubt and fading righteousness aside. This had to happen. He needed it to. No more room for Mr. Good Guy, not when it threatened to cost him the ultimate reward of claiming her for his own. For their own. Kane needed and wanted her as badly as Arawn did. His ploy wasn't selfish. It was survival for them both. The brief moment they contemplated losing her, he knew then and there his existence without her would be meaningless. No, if she would have them, they would take her. Tonight.

"My turn." He rushed back to the table, set down their glasses, tossed back his shot, and rejoined the game.

"Okay, let's see how close I can get to becoming a para-sandwich with you two stud muffins." She giggled.

Another wave of regret crashed over him. "Hey." Arawn sat on the edge of the mat, disappointed with himself.

She glanced over. "What is it?"

"I can't believe I'm about to say this, but...." He dipped his chin to his chest in shame.

"Oh no, by the gods, did I completely misread signals here?" Her cheeks blazed red, and she inched out of her precarious position to sit on the mat. She covered her face with her palms and shook her head.

"No, not at all. Don't get me wrong. I'm all for this," Arawn stammered. "It's everything I want, and more."

"But?"

Arawn hated that he'd made her sad. "Look, it's been a rough go for you. I want to be sure this isn't something you're going to regret."

"He does have a point, Trinity. I've started to feel pretty guilty myself," Kane confessed. "We really like you. The last thing we want to do is take advantage of you in a vulnerable situation."

Chapter Eleven

Trinity glanced back and forth between her immortal and her gargoyle's guilt-ridden stares. *Take advantage of me! Please!* "I won't lie, I've been conflicted for many reasons, but this draw I feel to both of you is more than I can take."

"We know you've been through so much." Kane rubbed her shoulder.

"To be honest, mourning my uncle has me terrified to move on, to connect with anyone else. I figured if I didn't get close, it would save me heartache." She tucked her knees up to her chest. "Does that make me a bad person?"

"Not at all." Arawn reached over and caressed her cheek. "How long has it been since he...?"

"Six months."

"It's gonna take time for you to heal. It's okay." Kane raked his fingers through his auburn locks.

"I know." Trinity's breath hitched. Uncle Connor would rise from the grave if he could just to tell her not to use his death as an excuse not to live. He sure as Tartarus had lectured her about it since her parents died.

Maybe it was the warmth of the licorice liqueur

spreading down her solar plexus and rolling over the ache in her muscles, or perhaps the sense of safety she felt with these two. But the cold exterior she had worked so hard to display melted away.

"I haven't avoided you both because of my grief."

"What is it, then?" Arawn traced his thumb over her bottom lip.

"With all that's happened around me these past months, I feel like I've lost my mind. I didn't want to get close and risk either of you getting hurt because of me." Her stomach tensed with her confession.

"Nothing will to happen to us, princess." Arawn kissed her forehead.

"The last person I cared for died a horrible death, and I still don't know why, but I feel like it had something to do with me." She hugged her legs tight to her chest and rested her chin on one knee.

"Hey." Kane shifted closer and sat in front of Trinity. "We've both been around death and suffering. A ton of it. You've seen the tattoos." He nodded to Arawn. "There was a long time we both felt responsible for the pain and harm that came to those who were loyal to us in the Underworld."

"Kane's right." Arawn scrubbed his face with his palms. "My father is a vicious bastard who tortured and murdered many. When we rose up against him, the Underworld divided like nothing I've ever seen before. Parents against children, siblings, mates. Many fought, some died, and others were captured and subjected to ferocious retribution." He paused and shook his head, his dark eyes glistening with sorrow.

Kane cleared his throat. "In time, we came to accept. We weren't the ones who caused the harm, so we stood up and put an end to it. None of us, including you, Trinity, are responsible for the actions of malevolent beings, supernatural or mundane. Free will is exactly that. No matter how much protection we offer, nothing will change the intention of the ones who do the harm."

Despite their previous admissions of their jaded pasts, Trinity had no idea how much these protectors had witnessed and endured. If anyone really was capable of comprehending her pain, it would be her immortal and her gargoyle.

"You're both right." She shifted and sat crossed legged. "I have another confession to make."

"Tell us." Arawn prodded.

"I held back, and tonight, might still have. Even though I despise those sadistic Bitches of Eastwick, I'm thankful for one thing."

"Being?" Kane nodded.

"When they taunted me in the dinner hall, they spiked a real jealous streak in me. No matter how much I denied my attraction to you both, I had to come to terms with it because of them...while in the process of being driven crazy." She shrugged.

"Wow," they stated in unison.

"Thanks to the trio, then." Arawn got up and poured another round.

"Okay." Trinity shook her shoulders to dispel the entirely too serious moment. "I'll make you both a deal." She lifted her chin and flashed a mischievous grin.

"Such as?" Kane rubbed her knee.

"I won't make it easy for either of you." She winked. "As you can see, I'm limber and determined. It's time to live and enjoy what life has to offer. But if either of you expects to get anywhere with me tonight, you'll have to win first. Consider it game on."

"What happens if you win?" Arawn returned with the filled tumblers and grinned.

"Well then, I'll have to have a shower, by myself, and settle in the great big bed over there, all by my lonesome, while you"—she pointed to Arawn—"sleep on the pullout, and you" she pointed to Kane—"perch up on the roof again."

"Ouch! Cold, Trinity, very cold." Kane feigned a shiver as he rubbed his bulging biceps.

"I'm sorry, but it's the way it has to be. I'm a fierce competitor." She narrowed her eyes. "I have to warn you, neither of you stand a chance."

"Oh, you think so?" Arawn folded his arms across his bulky chest. "What if one of us wins?"

"Oh, that's still going to take some work on your parts." She pursed her lips. "You won't get off easy, either way."

"How so?" Kane cocked his head.

"Well, once the game is over, you'll have to pamper me. Perhaps we will start with a massage, a shower, and then you plaster your lips all over my body...."

"Talk about a lack of motivation." Arawn tossed back his drink. "Let's up the ante, or we three fierce competitors might be at this game all night."

"Your proposal would be?" Anything that could create the need to land on top of him, of them, would definitely improve the game.

"For each move, we have another shot."

"I like the way you think, old friend." Kane rubbed his palms together and flashed a wicked grin.

"You're both on." Trinity sucked back her shot and set her glass at the side of the mat. "Positions, boys."

Once they got back into the places they left off, Arawn took the lead. The start had been easy; each of them squatted in their corner of the mat, no contact yet. He hoped that would change soon. A few more spins, three more rounds, and next came Trinity's turn. The sweet warmth of licorice trickled down Arawn's sternum and into his stomach.

"Your go, darlin'," Kane prompted her.

With her hands crossed over one another, her left foot in front, and her right foot to the green dot angled behind her, she carefully reached her right hand back and spun the needle.

"Ha! Right foot, red." Arawn crooned. He occupied the red side, which meant she would have to cross her back leg and thread it through his to keep playing. He ached for the chance to have her body rest up against his. Even if this was a childish ploy to get close to her, she was having fun, and it worked.

Trinity persevered and managed to maneuver into position with ease, to his astonishment. "Wow, you really are agile."

"You have no idea." She giggled.

"I'd like to." The words slipped past his loose lips before he could catch them. "Sorry."

"Don't be." Trinity shot him a wanton gaze.

"Uh..." Arawn found himself at a loss. Usually, he had a decent amount of confidence, but not only did this woman make his cock strain against the confines of his zipper, she disintegrated his tough, boastful façade.

"My go." Kane glared at the spinner far out of his reach. "Hey, darlin', do a gargoyle a favor and give it a spin for me?"

Trinity reached over and flicked the thin black needle. "Ha ha, left hand, blue." She giggled. "I'd like to see how you'll manage this move without falling. I'm completely in your way."

Arawn watched his buddy's face light up as he placed his feet and moved in for contact. Kane swung his left hand over Trinity, curled his arm around her waist, and placed his palm on the elusive blue dot under her ass. Now, he effectively cradled her contorted curves in his arms, which left him face to face with the coveted beauty. A twinge of envy rushed through Arawn when he caught her smile of acceptance.

Trinity's cheeks flushed bright red. "You were right," she murmured to Kane.

"About what, darlin'?"

"This is getting complicated." She bit her lower lip. "Arawn?" She peeked over Kane's shoulder.

"Yeah?"

"I could go for another shot."

"I'm on it." He inched out of position, not entirely sure he could get back in and not knock the lot of them down.

Arawn poured three more shots at the side of the mat. "Ladies first." He knelt beside her and held the rim of the glass to her lips.

The pupils of Trinity's pupils expanded, leaving a slim ring of the luminous blue. The corners of her mouth curved up into a naughty grin. She parted her lips and waited for him to feed her the drink. As he began to empty it, she eased her head back and let the liqueur spill onto her chin. It drizzled down her throat to her chest and settled into the delectable crevice of her burgeoning cleavage.

"Oopsie." Trinity moaned. "Now we've gone and made a sticky mess. With my hands busy, how will I ever get this off me?" Kane let out a low growl of excitement. "Are you sure?" he rasped as he hovered above her mouth with his. "Does this mean you forfeit?"

"I'm sure I want both of you to help." She stuck the tip of her tongue out and traced the outline of

Kane's lips and retreated. She glanced to Arawn and motioned him closer with her head. "Quit isn't in my vocabulary, but I want to play a grown-up game now. Come here, you big lug."

Arawn's cock stiffened at her melodic voice. He inched closer to her, ready to finally taste her kiss. Another urge he had been itching to scratch took hold first. "May I?" He motioned to her hair.

Trinity nodded. He unfastened the bun and let down her thick mane, finally. As he had envisioned, her white locks spanned the length of her back and dangled around her waist.

"Beautiful." He threaded his fingers through the silky strands and fanned the curls out. "I've wanted to do that since you first straddled me."

Trinity lifted her chin and gazed at him. He couldn't take it anymore and descended on her lips with his. Her sweet, decadent lips, so plump and inviting, and her talented tongue curled and danced with his.

Kane growled and shifted. "This is getting hard to hold."

Their banshee pulled back and laughed. "Your arms must be sore." She plunked her ass down on the mat and Arawn cradled her in his grasp.

"I wasn't referring to my arms." Kane got onto his knees and adjusted the front of his pants. "You've got me so stiff right now, it hurts."

"We can't have you in pain." She reached for his chest and tugged at his T-shirt.

Chapter Twelve

"**P**erhaps you can both help me get this mess cleaned up?" She motioned from her sticky chin down to her breasts.

"Should I get a cloth?" Arawn side-eyed her, uncertainty filling his rugged features.

"Aw, sweetheart, I think we're all out of cloths." She shook her head and pouted. "Try again...."

Kane let out a guttural growl and clambered to his hands and knees. "Any preference who and where, darlin'?"

"Whatever strikes your fancies," she cooed. "I'm yours for the taking."

"You might regret giving us free rein, beautiful." Arawn eased close and traced the tip of his tongue along her lips then sucked the licorice aphrodisiac from her chin.

The heat of his mouth sent ripples of excitement down her spine.

Kane moved in and licked the length of her throat and blazed a trail of fiery kisses down her chest. "Mmm, there seems to be something in my way." He glanced up with a wicked smirk then slipped a finger under the neckline of her sticky tank top and tugged it away from her. He gripped the material with both hands and tore it wide open, as easy as if it were tissue paper.

"Whoa." She chuckled with astonishment. "It wasn't my favorite anyway."

Kane reached his massive arms around her and unfastened her lace bra and freed her aching breasts. The delightful aroma of citrus, nutmeg and bergamot wafted up her nose. "Mmm," she cooed. *Armani, one of my favorites.* He whisked her left nipple with his skilled tongue, causing desire to curl around her spine.

"I hope he doesn't get to have all the fun," Arawn breathed into her ear. He nipped gently at her lobe.

"I'm all for equal rights," she declared with desperation. This was really happening. She surprised herself with how naturally she responded to their touch. It had been a long while since she was intimate with anyone, supernatural, or mundane.

Cupping the nape of her neck, Arawn guided her back onto the Twister mat, which left her open to their sweet invasion.

Kane continued his delicious assault on her nipples, and Arawn slid his finger inside the elastic waist of her yoga pants.

"Hope these aren't your favorites, either." He flashed a one-sided grin and tore the pants open as easily as Kane had her shirt. He tossed the scrap of material to the side and worked his passionate lips down the length of her belly.

Left in her lace panties, she was putty in their hands, and their mouths. Trinity reached out beside her and flicked the spinner on the game. "Your turns." She trembled with excitement. "Shirts and pants off."

They complied with her demand and tugged their T-shirts off. At last, she got to admire their flesh canvases of artwork all over again, only this time it would be every glorious inch of them. Her breath hitched when Arawn stood and unbuckled his belt. The clank of the metal shot a flutter of anticipation through her core. He pushed his cargo pants down his lean hips, dropped them to the floor, and quickly discarded them, along with his boxer briefs. Trinity licked her lips at the spectacular view of his distended cock, already fully erect and massive. To her other side, Kane had gotten to his feet and taken off his clothing as well.

"Oh, my," was all she could muster.

They knelt on either side of her and laid her down gently. Arawn inched her panties over her curvy hips as she watched him. "Do you even know how sexy you are?" he growled and skimmed his fingers along her thighs.

Trinity's cheeks burned with excitement, and, yet, shyness rolled over her with his words. "You don't have to say those kind of things...."

"We know." Kane skirted his palm along her belly and up her chest. "Sometimes you need to be told what we're thinking, instead of trying to read it." He cradled her neck with his palm while he pressed his lips to hers with an all-consuming kiss. The zesty sting of sweet licorice layered her mouth as she welcomed his tongue.

"Tell me, princess." Arawn crawled toward her feet. "Are you still limber?"

She released Kane's lips to respond. "I think so." She giggled. "Why?"

"Because I want to wrap your legs around my neck."

Without waiting for her reply, he lifted her feet and tucked them over his broad shoulders as he nestled between her thighs. Arawn caressed her bare pussy with his warm hand and slid his fingers along her slick folds.

Before she could moan with excitement, Kane claimed her lips again, with more urgency. He brushed the knuckles of his free hand along her jaw and down to her right breast. Their tongues intertwined while he pinched and rolled her swollen nipple between his fingertips. He cupped and kneaded her breast then bestowed his affection on the left one.

Arawn massaged her clit in delicious circles with his gifted tongue and dipped a finger inside her pussy. He massaged her inner walls with a talent she hadn't anticipated. Trinity panted, every nerve ending ablaze with fiery lust, and her rapid pulse thrummed behind her ears.

"Kane," she let out with a winded breath.

"Yeah, darlin'?"

"I want to taste you."

Her gargoyle shifted around and knelt above her head. He stared at her with his incredible emerald eyes that melted her insides like hot butter. Kane leaned over and kissed across her neck as he slid his other hand up underneath her back and gripped her skin tight.

Trinity reached her hand above her head and scraped her nails along the taut skin of Kane's tummy and then eased farther down and palmed his rigid cock. She slid her right hand along her stomach until she could grab a handful of Arawn's thick hair. She arched her back as he darted his tongue in and out of her throbbing pussy and massaged her clit with a frantic finger.

She tilted her head back. There, dangling over her famished lips, her snack was within reach. She brought the tip close and ran her tongue around the stiff ridge. Kane let out a throaty growl. She licked around the head, found the salty pre-cum, spread it around with her thumb then lapped it up. Trinity cradled his massive head on her tongue and accepted him farther into her mouth. He bucked deeper and dropped his palms on the game mat on either side of her.

"Fuck, you're amazing." He groaned.

She worked his length with her palm and her mouth, rhythmic and determined, but lost her focus when the onslaught of white hot ripples of electricity arced out from her clit.

"That's it, come for me, baby." Arawn sucked her clit and rammed his fingers in and out. "Fuck, you taste so sweet." His husky voice curled through her. The walls of her pussy convulsed. She gripped Arawn's hair tight as he dove deeper with his mouth. Trinity screamed with ecstasy between mouthfuls of Kane's cock. Every muscle in her body spasming, she arched her back as the dizzying explosion rocked her to the very core.

Kane pulled his cock back and claimed her lips with a devastating kiss. She exploded into a thousand pieces with both their mouths on her body.

"I want you," she pleaded with desperation.

"Which one, darlin'?" Kane traced his thumb over her bottom lip.

"Both of you, now," she begged.

Kane got to his knees and scooped her up into his grasp. He headed toward the bedroom and Arawn followed them.

Trinity wrapped her arms around Kane's muscular neck. "Let me down," she panted.

He did as she asked. Arawn hovered so close to her she could almost taste his lips. She stepped to her immortal and pressed her hands against his tattooed chest. His heart pounded hard and fast against her palms. She pushed at him until he backed up to the wall.

"What is it, gorgeous?" He tilted his head with confusion.

Trinity grinned and crouched down to admire his fully extended cock. She ran her palm along the inside of his thighs and cupped his balls. With her other hand, she grasped his steely shaft and leered up at him as she licked her lips and then fed the head of his cock slowly into her mouth. Groaning, he dipped his head back. Trinity savored her fleshy treat and took him in deeper with each stroke.

Arawn growled and jerked back from her mouth. "You're gonna make me come fast if you keep doing that."

"I hope so." She returned to feast on him with determination.

"I want to fuck you, Trinity...please?" Arawn braced his stance against the wall.

Trinity gripped his waist and rose to her feet then wrapped her arms around his neck. She tilted her chin up and kissed him. He lifted her under the arms and she wrapped her legs around his lean hips.

"Kane," she rasped. "Come here."

Arawn leaned his shoulders against the wall with her clinging to his hips. The length of his massive cock pressed against the folds of her swollen pussy. Kane approached from behind and blazed a trail of fiery kisses along the back of her neck and shoulders, his erection skimming the cheek of her ass. He grazed his teeth along her shoulder and bit gently.

With each kiss, nip of her skin, and tender touch, her juices coated her thighs. Kane slid his fingers over her swollen pussy and spread her wetness over her anus, priming her for the ultimate game point of the night. Arawn massaged her clit again, and her thighs jerked with his touch.

Kane cupped her tits in his palms, and Arawn gripped her ass cheeks.

Staring into the depths of her immortal's dark eyes, Trinity reached down between her legs, gripped the head of Arawn's cock, and positioned it, ready for him. He gave a long, slow thrust upward and plunged deep inside her. She cried out with elation. He filled her with every inch, while dark, delicious pleasure fluttered throughout her core. Arawn captured her mouth with hungry urgency.

She grasped Kane's hand and eased it down to her back. He continued to moisten her anus and then slipped a finger inside. Her breath hitched at the stinging sweetness. He worked his finger and inserted a second, the surreal bliss making her want more.

"Take me, Kane," she panted between frantic kisses from her immortal while she rode his rigid flesh. Pressure built inside her pussy. Her muscles tightened with every stroke.

Kane replaced his fingers with the tip of his hardness and gently eased in. Arawn pushed up deep inside her pussy and held her onto him as her gargoyle worked himself farther inside her ass, inch by inch.

"More," she begged, and he slid all the way in. "It feels so good," she huffed with pleasure.

Both men completely filled her. She angled her pelvis as she gripped Arawn's shoulders and inched herself up and down on their thick staffs. They followed her rhythm, and both thrust long and deep inside her. Arawn slipped a hand between them and rubbed her swollen clit. Kane cupped her tits in his massive hands and rolled her hardened nipples between his fingers.

Jolts of electricity shot down her spine and throughout her muscles. "Oh, by the gods, I'm...I'm...."

"Yes." Arawn growled and kissed her harder.

"I'm going to come with you," Kane rasped in her ear. He gripped her hair at the base of her scalp and pulled gently.

"Oh, yes!" The rough play spurred her on. "Harder!"

They rocked together in sensual tempo, their pace increasing, their breaths growing ragged. Arawn worked her clit to another frenzy of simultaneous explosions that spanned over her muscles and clenched deep inside her. Her pussy clamped down hard on his shaft, and she cried out as she came with soul-shattering intensity.

"Aw, baby, I feel you coming," Arawn uttered with punctuated gasps. "So tight." He slammed up harder and faster.

Both men collided into her with perfect rhythm while she rode wave after wave of her glorious peak. Her immortal let out a hoarse growl then stiffened in release as he pressed deep inside her.

"Fuck!" Kane gripped her hip with one hand, tugged on her hair with the other, and pounded her ass even harder. "Oh, yeah," he roared and bit down on her neck like a wild animal claiming his mate as he pushed deep and came wildly inside her.

Trinity shuddered with a chain of spasms, pressed tight between their shaking bodies. They panted for air, and she savored every sensation of their masculine moans of satisfaction, how they pulsed deep inside her, and how they both held her tight as the three of them tremored with completion.

Chapter Thirteen

Kane took Trinity's hand and led her to the bathroom. "We promised you a shower. We always keep our promises."

True to form, Sage had left a plethora of colored, fragrant candles on the long marble sink counter top, alongside a basket with matches, soaps, towels, and facecloths. Kane lit the candles to set the ambiance in the spacious room. The brief odor of sulfur from the match wafted up his sensitive gargoyle nose, soon replaced by the delectable scents of vanilla, jasmine, and cinnamon. He headed to turn on the water. The luxurious shower had a wide glass door, white porcelain tiles, wall-mounted multi-directional jets, a large rain showerhead above, and enough room for the trio, with a convenient bench on the far wall.

Trinity remained quiet, her alabaster face flushed from their high-intensity romp. "You're so fucking beautiful." Kane brushed her loose hair back from her eyes and kissed her luscious lips. "Hey." He pulled back and studied her. "You okay, darlin'?"

She gave an emphatic nod. "Better than okay." She nuzzled into his chest. "I'm happy."

"Come here." He stepped into the steamy shower and held out his hand to her. "Hey, Arawn, you gonna join us?"

"Oh, Tartarus, yeah." Arawn pulled out towels and set them on the handrail beside the shower. He grabbed body wash and a face cloth from the wicker baskets on the marble countertop and followed them in.

"What took you so long?" Trinity glanced at him.

"Had to get the feeling back in my legs. That was...."

"Incredible." Kane finished his sentence.

"That's one word for it." He pulled the glass door shut behind him and planted a feathery kiss on Trinity's lips. Then, he opened the bottle and poured a generous amount of soap on the face cloth, lathered it up, and caressed their banshee's shoulders and down her back while she faced Kane.

"I do recall," Kane grumbled, "you're supposed to get some rest tonight. You've got a big day ahead of you tomorrow."

"I'm more relaxed and clear minded than I've been in months. I promise, I will sleep soon." She plastered her hands on his chest and glanced over her shoulder at his friend. "Besides, I can't let you break your promise."

"Fair enough, princess." Arawn chuckled. "But be forewarned. We could easily be convinced to continue this all night." He glided the soapy cloth up to her neck and down her chest.

"I think we'll have to show some restraint before sunrise." Kane growled. His dick stiffened against her belly when she leaned closer to him. With a lathered palm, she stroked his cock and then let the warmth of the cascading water trickle over it.

"You may, but I can't guarantee I will," she cooed. Their banshee stepped to the side and sat on the tiled bench. Steam filled the air and wrapped around her voluptuous form. "Front and center, you two."

They did as she asked, and she reached for Kane first. She palmed his shaft with a slippery grip. Trinity released him, to his protest, but then cupped her tits and pressed them together. Kane licked his lips at the erotic invitation and stuck his cock between her creamy mounds. The sensational pressure against his flesh as she stroked his cock between her breasts shot tingles along his spine; his balls tightened. Their banshee stared up at him, and she stroked him to the brink of eruption—how quickly he peaked. Kane let out a throaty growl and exploded between her tits.

Arawn got the same delightful treatment. After more lather and steamy shower, they soon whisked her off to bed.

Kane took a place on the far end of the bed and held out his hand for her to join him in the middle. She snuggled up close to him, and Arawn took his place on her other side. He pulled the blankets over her curves and smoothed his palm down the cotton shield.

"After you're asleep, I'll take point on the roof while you both get some rest." He kissed her forehead.

A frown tainted her beautiful face. "You won't stay the night?"

"I would, darlin', but we still have to keep you safe." Kane stroked her damp hair back from her eyes. "Arawn will sleep next to you. Perhaps after you're done with your trip to the Elysian Fields, I can get a nap with you tomorrow."

"Fine, but I'll hold you to it."

Trinity turned on her side, with her back to

Arawn, settled between them, and closed her eyes. Arawn spooned her and dozed off within minutes. Kane watched their sleeping beauty between them with amazement. How fortunate had they been? After all Trinity had been through, she still managed to trust them and let them close to her.

He listened to the soft sounds of her breathing as she slumbered. It took every ounce of strength he had not to fall asleep beside her. Instead, he indulged for what seemed to be an hour of quiet admiration at her side. Her skin was flawless, her brows fine and perfectly shaped, and her luscious mouth still beckoned him after a full night of passionate lovemaking. He leaned down and planted a feathery kiss on her delightfully swollen lips. She didn't stir. He took solace in how sound she slept.

In the same position he had been since they'd lain down, tension filled his stomach. His acute hearing kicked in. The silence outside was bested by a distant rumble of thunder. He turned and glanced out the window. Brief flashes lit up the sky. Something was coming, but it was far more than mere rain. Darkness took hold of his keen senses. He tapped Arawn who bolted upright in an instant. Kane pointed to his eye and motioned toward the window—their signal for *I'm going to check this out*—and eased the covers off.

They slipped out of bed, covered her curves with the blanket, and darted to the living room where their clothes lay scattered. He pulled on his boxers and pants. Kane snatched the handheld radio. His shoulder blades burned with caution.

"Stay with her. I'll go outside and call in and see what's happening."

"Go," his comrade concurred.

Kane unlocked the door and shinnied up the porch pillar to the rooftop. Although his shift was an instinctive response when he detected danger, he warded off the change, fearful of their banshee seeing him in that form. He scanned the dark stillness along the water line, and back to the island. His gargoyle senses screamed trouble, but his acute vision and sense of smell picked up nothing.

He clicked the button on the radio and called out. "Checkpoint, all posts, over?"

The radio crackled, but no reply. "Checkpoint, does anyone copy? This is Kane."

More crackles resonated, and then a voice sounded. "Yeah, Kane, this is Rekkus. What's wrong?"

"I'm not sure...but something is up. There's a storm brewing over the water."

"We heard it, too. Any sign of the Dread Ones?" Rekkus replied.

"Negative." Kane released the button and waited for direction.

"All units, this is team leader, sound off location and status, over." Rekkus' tone was stern but calm.

"Check point one, all is clear here."

"Check point two, nothing to report."

Eight units sounded off, but no one had spotted anything unusual. Kane's gut knew different. He waited for the final two to respond, but they didn't. A blinding bolt of lightning lit the black sky, and a thunderous crack boomed in the air. Residual tremors of the long rumbles shook the roof he stood on.

"Unit nine, sound off," Rekkus demanded.

They didn't reply. Kane lifted his head and drew in a long whiff of the dry air. No threat of rain, but vicious flashes repeatedly filled the entire sky. Horrific cracks of thunder pierced his sensitive ears. Kane scouted the landscape and the water for any sign of danger. Not a single gust of wind, yet the clouds rolled by like a speeding train. Out of nowhere, a torrential downpour started and then shifted to horizontal rain with blasts of wind of epic proportions. More cracks of lightning bolts lit the sky. The gusts hit in solid waves, so fierce it nearly knocked the rock-solid gargoyle off his feet. A brutal fireworks display of nature threatened to strike close. Another crack of lightning hit a tree at the forest beside the dock. Kane jumped down from the roof in a single leap and ducked inside the cabin.

"What is it?" Trinity stood, draped in a sheet, with Arawn's arms wrapped around her trembling body.

"It's just a thunderstorm," he lied. He caught Arawn's stare and feigned a lighthearted shrug.

The cabin lights flickered then blacked out, and everything went deathly silent. The rain, thunder, and lightning all stopped, and the lights flickered back on.

"What in Tartarus...?" Arawn hissed.

"Kane, do you read me?" a different voice rang out from the radio.

"This is Kane," he called back.

"It's Cemil. I'm at the barracks. Everything is okay."

"What happened?" Rekkus hollered into the radio.

"I'm with Brody Natura," Cemil sounded winded.

"This was Brody?" Rekkus roared.

"Yeah." The static increased. "He had a nightmare. It's under control now."

"You've got to be kidding." Arawn widened his eyes. "The teen with kinetic abilities," he murmured in a low voice to a visibly stunned Trinity. "He's had trouble with his talents, hasn't been able to control them."

"I can relate." She flashed a weak grin.

"Copy that. Rekkus," Kane continued, "Be advised, there is one more unit not checked in." Adolescent nightmare or not, his gut kept him on alert.

"Unit nine, sound off," Rekkus ordered.

Silence ensued for several seconds.

"Yes, sir, this is unit nine." The radio crackled.

"Where were you?" Rekkus snarled.

"The post we were at got struck by lightning, sir. No injuries, but we had to run for it."

"Damage report? All units," Rekkus demanded.

"Three trees down and a small blaze by unit nine, sir. It's under control now. Over."

The rest of the units checked in, casualty and damage free.

Trinity rushed to the bathroom, returning with a towel, and approached Kane. Worry shone in her bright-blue eyes as she patted down his soaked hair and face. "Did you get hurt?"

"No, darlin', I'm fine." He cupped her hand against his cheek and then kissed the inside of her wrist. "So much for a peaceful night." He grinned.

Chapter Fourteen

T he warmth of his body against her back eased Trinity from her restless sleep.

I so want to wake you up with me deep inside you. His naughty words filled her head and sent flutters of anticipation throughout her core.

"I'm not opposed to a morning stiffy." She giggled, her eyes still shut.

"What?" Surprise tainted Arawn's voice.

"You said you wanted to wake me up with you deep inside me. I'm all for it." She arched her back and pressed her ass against his hardness through the material of his pants.

"Trinity, I didn't say a word." His tone was tinged with alarm.

"You didn't?" She opened her heavy eyelids and turned over.

"No." He knitted his brows. "But those were my exact thoughts, word for word."

A loud thump sounded on the porch.

"Kane's up, too." Arawn propped his elbow on the pillow above her and threaded his fingers through her hair. With his free hand, he held her necklace between his fingers and frowned. "I think maybe the talisman is losing its protection."

"Right." In two days, she hadn't read a single thought of anyone on the island, and it had been such a relief, she hadn't anticipated the curse returning so quickly.

The front door opened, and Kane strolled in, stretching his arms over his head as he yawned. "Good morning."

"Morning." She forced a smile to greet him, despite the lingering fear festering in her stomach.

"Let's get you some coffee and breakfast." Her immortal squeezed her tight and kissed her forehead. "Cemil wants us to bring you to see Sarka first then to the Elysian Fields to meet him."

"Oh, okay." A sense of dread filled her chest.

What could Sarka want this time? Maybe she blamed Trinity for the teen's hellish nightmare last night? Although a conference with the dark Rowan sister held far more appeal than the prospect of a face-to-face confrontation with her parents or her uncle from the realm of the dead. She had pushed her worry aside for days. It had been convenient to forget her fear they might blame her for their deaths, or, worse yet, reveal she had gone insane after all.

Proof was in the pudding; even the temporary reprieve of magical jewelry hadn't been enough to stave her empathic curse. Just as she had experienced with Arawn a moment ago, her ability to read thoughts had returned, a talent that would once again prove torturous on the island with other paras and humans alike. How long would it be before she became subject to bouts of searing pain in her head again? Overpowered with others' emotions?

"Hey, princess." Arawn cradled her cheek in his palm and gazed into her eyes. "It'll be okay. Things will get better from here on out."

Trinity needed to believe him, but her pesky self-doubt overruled his words of comfort. She nuzzled her cheek into his hand and relished the affection and support.

Clad in jeans, a T-shirt, and runners, she tried to enjoy the hearty breakfast of sausage and eggs Kane whipped up for them. The trip in the golf cart to meet Sarka at the Haus proved to be a long, quiet one. Arawn drove and Kane sat on the back while she rode shotgun. The intensity of both their worries crowded her. Irritation flooded her at the invasion of uncertainty, theirs and her own.

Their arrival didn't alleviate the awkward silence. Her gargoyle held open the door, and she entered the main building with little enthusiasm. They approached the front desk to find Myron there to welcome them with a friendly smile.

"Good morning Miss McWraith." She flipped her cards.

"Trinity, please. Call me Trinity." She glanced at the name tag and shook her head with amusement. "Still can't find yours, huh, Geoff?"

"As fate would have it, not today, Trinity." Myron giggled. "Sarka is ready for you. You two gentlemen, Rekkus is doing a security check in the dining hall. He's waiting for you."

Trinity hugged herself as she avoided the dire need to touch or kiss her immortal and gargoyle. A sudden upsurge of shame washed over her at the realization they could get into serious trouble with the cranky tiger man if he found out about their three-way tryst. A tidal wave of insecurity struck.

What if, after this week, I never see them again? I'm not good enough for them, except for a single night of fucking. They got laid; maybe they'll ask to be reassigned and be done with me. What was wrong with her? Last night, she had been relaxed, confident, and felt so much at ease with them both. Where did this plethora and negative emotions come crashing in from? They certainly hadn't done anything to ignite her angst. They had been sweet, caring, and affectionate, as they had been all week.

"Miss...uh, Trinity?" Myron snagged her attention away from her obsessive self-loathing.

"Um...yeah?" She shook her head to dispel the despair that had somehow encased her within seconds of being away from them.

"Are you all right?" Myron set her cards down and stood.

"Sure, why do you ask?"

"You seemed to drift off there for a minute." The receptionist stepped around the desk and escorted her to the office door. "Your eyes glazed, and you were somewhere else."

"I did?" Fogginess rolled over her brain.

"I'll see you in to Sarka, and I'll be right back, okay?" Panic filled Myron's mind. "Wait." Trinity gripped her arm with urgency. "You're afraid? Your chest hurts and you're nauseous?"

Myron's breath hitched. "Right this way, Trinity. Please, there is no time to waste."

She complied mindlessly, her limbs numbed, and Myron led her to the door. It was as if she were in a daydream. She could see, on autopilot, but had little control over her thoughts or body.

"Sarka," Myron's tone held a tinge of the same panic Trinity sensed. "It's happening. The cards.... I have to get the others, as we discussed."

"Now?" Sarka met them at the door. Uncharacteristic anxiety filled her exotic features. "Yes, Myron. Go now. I've got her."

Relief and sorrow washed over Trinity when she

couldn't read Sarka. "What's happening to me?"

"I need you to look at me." Sarka cupped her chin and stared into her eyes. "Where are your glasses?"

Her breath caught in her throat. "I forgot them back at the cabin."

"It's okay. You're safe here." She shifted slightly to the side and recaptured Trinity's wandering gaze. "Where is your talisman?"

Her hands had numbed, her arms like Jell-O. "Around my neck."

"It's not there now. Think back. When do you last remember having it on?"

"We were on our way here."

"Did anything happen after the storm last night?"

"I don't think so. I didn't sleep well."

"What about this morning?"

"I woke up, I...." She searched her foggy brain. "I heard Arawn's voice when I woke up."

"He spoke to you?"

Trinity snapped out of the daze, a shockwave of terror sliced through her chest. "No, he was thinking. I heard his thoughts in my sleep. He said the necklace must have stopped working, but I had it on at the time."

"Did you take it off?" Sarka spoke with a stern tone.

"No. At least, I don't think so."

"Your talents are not blocked anymore. You're feeling everything all at once, like when you first arrived. In order to help you achieve balance, we had to mute the stimuli around you. That gave you a little break to build your strength."

Trinity knew exactly what Sarka meant. Soon, she would be overwhelmed with every thought, emotion, and concern they all had, which would leave her even more vulnerable to attack by the Furies. "Can't you bind my powers?"

"Which ones?"

"All of them?"

"Then who will you be? Your gifts are a part of you." Sarka shook her head. "To bind you is not a solution."

"It will take this damned target off of my back, won't it?"

"Bemoaning your genetic inheritance won't help you gain balance or control."

"Then what will?" Her eyes blurred with tears of frustration.

The office door burst open, and in came Rekkus, Cyrus, Kane, and Arawn.

"What happened?" Rekkus stormed to Sarka. "Myron said she saw them in the cards?"

"I'm not sure, but her talisman is gone," Sarka replied. "Did either of you see her take it off?"

"No," Kane replied.

"She had it on when she woke up." Arawn glanced around the floor as if trying to locate the object in question. "We had breakfast, she got dressed, and we came straight here." He paused. "But she heard my thoughts this morning. I wondered if it had stopped working."

"We need to treat this as a level one safety threat." Rekkus stated.

"I don't understand." Trinity scouted everyone's panicked expressions. "Someone, please explain to me what in Tartarus is going on? Why are you so hyper vigilant?"

"We communicated with higher sources to get some answers." Cyrus's nostrils flared as he spoke. "The Syndicate did not approve or support the Furies to be sent after you, so they will answer to their interference once they've been caught."

"So, then, who sent them?" she beseeched.

"We're still not sure, but if the Syndicate doesn't know about it, it's underground and runs deep, like Arawn suspected." Rekkus said.

Cyrus pressed his lips tight for a moment. "Last night's storm was no coincidence. Your symptoms and missing amulet confirms our suspicions. The Furies are on the attack as we speak."

Trinity heard murmurs from Arawn and looked to him for answers. He had leaned in to chat with Kane. "Tell me what you know, please?"

Arawn threaded his fingers through her hair, but the soothing touch he offered had no impact on her nerves that blazed with wrath. "The favor I called in, an acquaintance from the Underworld, confirmed there is a new movement going on. The information is minimal, but there is a hit list of paras under attack, and you're on it."

"There's more. Spill it."

"So were your parents, and your uncle," he confessed.

What could they have possibly done to warrant such a horrific fate? "Why?"

"We don't know. That's all the intel they could gather. Like we said, it runs deep." Arawn lowered his chin.

"So, how am I supposed to find out more?"

Sarka cleared her throat. "Cemil is waiting for you now. There's no time to waste. There are only three paras who can tell you what you need to know."

Trinity squeezed her eyes shut and cringed. "My dead family."

"Hey." Kane rubbed her shoulder. "You doin' okay, darlin'?" The soothing tone he offered did nothing to disguise the alarm his eyes held.

"No," she snarled and tugged away from his touch.

Red flooded her vision, and she stormed past the crowd and out the door.

"Wait!" several voices demanded.

Trinity bolted for the golf cart, determined to do this on her own. Mere steps away from the driver's seat, a sudden grip on her upper arm jerked her back and spun her around.

"Let me go," she wailed.

"Hey, princess." Arawn placed his palms on her cheeks and stared deep into her eyes. The warmth of his dark orbs smoothed out the venom coursing through her veins. She lowered her shoulders, and the boiling of her blood suddenly eased.

"What just happened?" She shrugged with defeat. "Why did I go into a fit of rage?"

"It's the Furies." He pulled her into his embrace and held together her shattering pieces. "They're messing with your mind. My guess is they need to weaken you before you get to the Elysian Fields."

"Why?" she whimpered and nestled into his powerful chest.

"If you get the answers you need, the closure and the healing, it takes away their leverage to torment you. They can't hurt you physically. Their power over you is psychological."

Kane rushed to them. "Is she okay?"

"I'm so sorry," she sobbed. Right back to the state of insecurity and devastation which consumed her before she arrived on the island, Trinity was crushed.

"Look at me," Kane commanded. She twisted her head to the side to find his brilliant emerald eyes filled with sadness. "They won't win. We won't let them hurt you anymore."

"I know you wouldn't," she disputed with helplessness.

"Then don't you dare let them either." His voice

held a dark command she'd never experienced with him before.

"What?" Arawn had been more of the aggressor of the two. This dominance was uncharacteristic of her gargoyle in her short experience with him.

"You're the most intelligent woman I've ever met." He stared her down, and his gaze softened. "They are not smarter than you. If you want to beat this, you need to lift your chin and stand tall."

"How?" The need to push away the terror and defeat was still heavily weighted by her trepidation.

"You've helped others with their emotions for years. How would you help a patient to overcome fear, adversity, or self-doubt?"

Trinity pondered his thought-provoking question. "I would get them to find their inner strength."

"Okay, what if they don't have any?" he bantered with a smartass smirk filling his rugged features.

"We all have inner strength...." As the words spilled from her lips, the realization of his logic sank into her weary brain. "I have the strength."

"You're not only the most intelligent, you're also the strongest woman I've ever met," Arawn concurred and released her from his embrace.

"You're right, both of you." Trinity steeled her back with purpose. "I'm not a victim." She shook her head. "Let's go. It's time to put an end to this mind-fuck." She hopped in the golf cart shotgun, and they headed out.

Chapter Fifteen

L ost in her conflicted internal dispute of dread crossed with rage, Trinity hadn't paid attention to the route they took until Arawn pulled to a stop. She glanced up to find the most breathtaking scenery—a vast forest of cedar, oaks, and birch trees, painted with the most whimsical floral carpet of lavender which stood two feet tall and swayed in the breeze.

"Welcome to the conduit to the Elysian Fields." Cemil approached the cart and greeted them.

"This is so beautiful," she whispered with astonishment.

Trinity climbed out of the vehicle and followed Cemil into the lush purple flowers. As they walked through the field of feathery lavender, she drew in the most delectable floral aroma. Some of the trees farther behind the cedar and oak were twisted and knotty with massive trunks, widths that would take four people to surround with joined hands to encircle. Magnificent blossoms of pink and red filled them. Trinity wandered away from her guide and inspected one closer. "These flowers look like baby dragons?"

"They're Dracaena Cinnabari, or better known as

ancient Dragon's Blood Trees. See the red sap that has dripped down the trunks?" The Rowan brother pointed.

"Yes." Trinity ran her finger over the sticky substance and sniffed the residue. The heady scent was a cross between a spicy lavender and fruity pine. She drew in another exhilarating inhale. "It's divine."

"The resin is used for medicine, incense, candles, and it's a powerful boost for any work with magic. This is Sarka and her coven's personal stash." Cemil grinned. "But don't tell her I said so."

Trinity glanced up at the monstrous umbrella shape of branches and leaves overhead. "The blossoms are exquisite."

"They're indigenous only to conduits that lead to the Elysian Fields. It's a telltale sign you're near a magical realm. Other places in the world where you would find Dragon's Blood trees, you'd never see these blossoms. They possess a magical essence which permeates the air and makes it viable to open the conduit to the Underworld."

The soft chirp of crickets sounded then, and, above, gentle notes of birds singing lulled her sense of worry. "I never knew that was possible?"

"It's one of our secret healing prospects on the island. Only to be used in dire situations where more traditional treatments don't help resolve the grief of losing loved ones."

"I've heard some myths of the Elysian Fields but never about what they really are." She glanced at her guide, hoping he'd elaborate.

"It's the final resting place of souls, for both the heroic and the virtuous."

Trinity's chest tightened, and her breath hitched.

"What's wrong?" Cemil cocked his head.

"My mother won't be here."

"Why do you think that?"

"She murdered my father and committed suicide. That annihilated any virtue she may have had." Anger churned in her belly.

Cemil offered a tender smile. "I'm sure the Fates would have a different view, given the Furies manipulated her, as they do with you now. I don't see you as any less virtuous. You're still kind, caring, and compassionate to others."

His words almost held enough power to sway her train of thought, but the fear and doubt still enveloped her.

A low growl echoed to the left of them, in the depth of the trees. She caught a glimpse of a black shadow darting past some trees. Trinity swallowed hard against the lump in her throat.

"It's okay. It's Rekkus, and he's securing the parameter to make sure we're all safe." Arawn cupped the nape of her neck and gently rubbed her locked muscles.

"You're sure?"

"Look, see right there?" He pointed in the direction of a few trees from where she had fixed her stare.

Trinity followed the point of his finger to find a magnificent black tiger strolling out into the open, a majestic and extremely large were-cat. The protector gave a fierce roar, lifted his nose, and sniffed the air. He then let out a grunt and jetted back toward the tree line.

"All clear, according to the boss man." Kane chuckled.

"My apologies for any distress you suffered last night. Our young guest, Brody...." Cemil began to walk again, farther into the forest.

"Had a nightmare. I heard." Trinity held her hands

open and continued to follow him. The lavender flowers tickled her palms as she walked. The contact of her skin to the flowers released a sweet aroma that cloaked her with a sense of calm. "I can appreciate how he feels."

"I would have spent more time with you this week, to help sort out all of this sooner. He's had a difficult adjustment the past few months."

"Why?" Her curiosity piqued, or perhaps her inner therapist had finally reared its forgotten tendencies.

"I'm not permitted to disclose other guests' private information."

"Pardon me. I should know better." In her profession, it was the first rule when you treated any client.

"I can say," he offered, "*any* teen with emerging gifts, coupled with a recent loss, is bound to struggle." Cemil glanced back and winked.

"Gotcha." She nodded. "Where is he now?"

"He's taking a nap back at the barracks. We needed to keep him away from the Haus while he gets things under control, but last night, he didn't sleep well."

Technically, Cemil didn't breach confidentiality. He offered a generic statement about milestones and the obstacles they bring. Every teen, both para and human alike, faced similar challenges with hormonal shifts, but throw in new talents to contend with and, well, that in itself, was a mind-fuck for them, and the people around them.

They arrived at a cluster of five massive oak trees, and Cemil stepped to the side. Trinity approached and stared at the circular base of the trees, where a deep pool of teal water lay. The circumference of the water could easily fit three people like a luxurious hot tub.

"What is this?" She bent over and inspected it with fascination. A steam of pungent sweetness rushed over her face. "This smell is familiar, but I can't place it."

"Heather is a magical herb and assists in opening portals to the Underworld realm. Juniper is a protective herb that will intoxicate spirits into becoming visible, as well as increase your ability to see them. It's what makes the transition into the realm successful."

Trinity moved her hand above the water, tempted to dip her fingers in it.

Cemil gripped her wrist and prompted her back. "I wouldn't advise sticking your fingers in there."

"Why not?" She stood to face him.

"This is the cauldron for the conduit. It's magical, but there are only a few paras who can touch it. Those who can are essentially the key to unlock the door to the Underworld."

"And those who can't?"

"Consider it the extreme security system. Any unwanted visitors who touch or try to enter will perish."

"Perish as in...?"

"Spontaneously combust. Some have been said to be quite a spectacular fireworks display." Cemil pressed his lips tight.

"Burst into flames?" She plastered her palms to the sides of her thighs and forced a swallow.

"Arawn," Cemil continued, "I need your help to open the conduit, and then you both have to wait here with me."

"We're going with her." Kane wrapped his arm around her shoulder in a show of protection.

"I'm afraid that's not possible, big guy." Cemil shook his head. "Only the blood descendent or the grief-stricken can enter for the purpose of healing and closure."

"But her safety?" Kane challenged. Trinity glanced up to catch his cheeks burn red. "She's in danger. We have to protect her."

"It's part of the agreement we made with Hades, so we can have this access to the Underworld, solely for the purpose to send those in dire need to the Elysian Fields. This is the first time we've actually had cause to use this in all our time here on the island. It's non-negotiable. If we break the rules, the conduit will be closed to us forever."

"First time?" Trinity recoiled with fright. "I'm a guinea pig?"

"Don't worry, you're in good hands." Cemil winked.

Arawn patted Kane on the shoulder. "No one else can enter, not even the Furies. She'll be safe in there. It's out here that she is vulnerable to attack."

Kane held her close and kissed her forehead. "We'll be right here."

Trinity bit her lip. Nerves clawed at her insides as panic surfaced. She forced her breathing to slow in a vain attempt to ease her rapid pulse thrumming behind her ears. "Will it hurt?"

"No." Arawn shook his head. "It's kind of like floating in a blissful daydream, only the mental clarity is unlike anything you've ever experienced."

"What should I say?" She shook her head and looked to Cemil, her mind racing with fear and confusion.

"Whatever feels right at the time. There is no way to prepare to see a loved one who has passed." The fair-haired Rowan brother knitted his brows. "This journey is about finding peace. Whatever is needed to help you achieve closure will naturally unfold. Trust in the gods."

"Easy for you to say. You're not on a para hit list," she mumbled.

"Actually, we are."

Chapter Sixteen

Trinity watched as Arawn knelt at the base of the cauldron. He closed his eyes and held his palms above the pool of water.

"Why is Arawn able to do this?" she whispered to Kane.

"One of his talents is the control over magical cauldrons. In the Underworld, he has the power to restore youth and healing from his father's cauldron to those deemed worthy."

"Has he ever done this before?" Steam intensified and the water began to swirl like a whirlpool.

"Not here, no."

"What if he gets...?" She reached out for him. "Stop!"

"It's okay," Cemil assured her.

Trinity hugged herself tight as she watched. Beads of perspiration streamed down her immortal's temples, and he rocked back and forth, keeping his eyes clenched shut. His breathing increased. He crinkled his sweat-soaked forehead, and his outreached hands shook as the force of the swirling water intensified. Arawn's face flushed dark red, and he rasped, "It's time, go now, Trinity." He maintained his concentration. The velocity of the water accelerated, the swirl in the pool deepened, and the center lowered into a hole.

"How?" She shook her head, terrified to move.

"Jump," Cemil called over the gusts of wind encircling them. "It won't hurt, I promise you." He gripped her shoulders and guided her to stand on the curved tree truck in front of her. "Feet first. Hurry. He can't hold this for long."

Trinity glanced back to her gargoyle to find a forced smile. "It's okay, darlin'," he hollered over the noise of the conduit. "We'll be right here, waiting for you."

With that, Trinity squeezed her eyes shut and jumped into the hollowed water turnstile. Her stomach bottomed out as she fell hard and fast. She opened her eyes to find her plummet swift and unyielding. She couldn't fix her sights on anything as it zoomed past. Dark soil and rock soon transformed to vivid red. Swirls of bright light and orange glows mixed and tightened around her. It quickly encased her like a billowy blanket and slowed her speed. Within seconds, she caught glimpses of tree tops and greenery below. The energy field of warmth and safety brought her to the grassy surface with a gentle touchdown, and she landed on her feet.

As quickly as she dropped, the energy field retreated upward and then evaporated. She glanced around and steadied her wobbly knees as her stomach churned from the warp-speed descent. Trinity took in her surroundings—a perfect extension of the exquisite conduit she had just wandered through. The Elysian Fields held the identical Dragon's Blood trees with dragon blossoms, a majestic forest of green blanketed with the very same sensational floral carpet of tall lavender swaying in the gentle breeze. High up, among sporadic clouds, shone the vibrant sun, just like the surface above. The only difference was, she was alone, and for the first time in days, completely free of fear, panic, and dread. Calm and serenity washed over every muscle.

Beside her stood the same cluster of trees with the pool of water at the base. Only the water glowed a shimmering gold, not teal. Steam rose and encircled a translucent form. Trinity fixed her gaze on the shifting image materializing before her. A man stood tall, more than a foot taller than her immortal and gargoyle. A dark, brooding man with piercing sea-green eyes and long ebony hair cascading over his broad shoulders stepped away from the cauldron. Draped in a regal toga of white with bronze embroidery and a three-point crown of shiny black onyx, he had the noble presence of an ancient Greek god.

"Who are you?" Her voice was but a whisper.

"I am Hades, son of Cronus, Ruler of the Dead and Keeper of the Elysian Fields." This being held no hint of humor or hospitality, instead, he presented a stern glare. In his left hand, he held a tall wooden scepter with dark crystals pointing out of the top,

"By the gods...." She dropped to her knees and bowed.

"Your worship is not necessary here. You have a special request?"

"I-I need...." Her lip quivered, the words wouldn't come out.

"You need closure with your loved ones. Yours is a difficult situation?"

"It is." She clambered to her feet and dipped her chin.

"There is no need for shame or humility. Cast your eyes upon me, Trinity."

She snapped her head up with shock. "You know

who I am?"

"I do. We have been expecting you." He waved his hand toward the tree line.

"We?"

"There is not much time. This is the land of the dead, not the living. Complete your business and you must be gone soon."

Trinity followed the direction of his hand to find a familiar figure approaching in the distant field.

She glanced back to Hades, but he had vanished.

"Trinity," the voice she knew from her childhood called out. He stepped into the sunlight.

"Daddy?"

Dressed in a similar but less impressive toga, he stood with his long white hair cascading down his back. She traipsed through the flowers to reach him, the urgent need to race into his outreached arms growing with each step. Halting just a few feet away from him, shock washed over her at the virile image of her father. He stood before her, young and healthy, the radiance of his pale skin contrasted against his glistening azure eyes. A single tear spilled down his cheek. The final memory she had of him encased a bloody massacre she'd never recovered from.

"My sweet baby girl," he whimpered and scooped her up into a warm hug. "By the gods, how I've missed you."

Trinity sank into his embrace. She clutched him tight as relief and joy radiated in her chest. "You're all right."

"Of course I am. This is a place of peace, free from harm and sadness." He released her and stepped back, studying her from head to toe, beaming with paternal pride. "You have grown into a beautiful woman, with such a pure heart and soul. I'm so very proud of you."

Trinity dropped her gaze to the ground. She folded her hands in front of her as guilt permeated her brain.

"What is it, sweetheart?" Her father cupped her cheek.

"The night I cried for your death...."

"Listen to me, baby." He prompted her by the chin to meet his adoring gaze. "You were only six. You had no way to know what it meant. I am so sorry for the burden it has placed on you for all these years."

Sorrow and doubt flooded her chest. "Could I have saved you, Daddy?"

"No, you couldn't have. The banshee wail is never intended to save but to provide warning so people can bid farewell to their loved ones."

"Is that why you sent me away with Uncle Conner?"

"Yes. To lose both parents at such a young age was a travesty in itself, but to have been witness to it, I couldn't bear to have you endure that." He shook his head and more tears spilled down his face.

"But I did." The resentment she had carried all these years still festered in her gut, layered with sorrow and dread.

"I know, my darling. It wasn't my wish for you, but the Fates have wisdoms far beyond what we are able to see." He swiped away the wetness and sucked in a deep breath. "They have a grand plan for all, and part of your destiny was to see and to be protected."

"Why?" Tears stung her eyes. "Tell me the purpose of Mother...doing that to you. How could she? You loved her so." Trinity sobbed.

"All of your questions will be answered, but know this right now." He held her face between his heated palms. "We both love you. The anger and the hatred you harbor because of your grief has weakened you and makes you vulnerable. At this very moment, you are in danger."

"With the Furies, I know, Father."

"The danger lies beyond the Furies, I'm afraid."

"What do you mean?" She cupped her hand against his and nuzzled his palm, relishing the contact she had longed for.

"There is much to share, but the story is not all mine to tell." He glanced over his shoulder, where another man with short, blond hair and dark-blue eyes stood. "Time is short, and we have much to resolve before you must leave."

"Uncle Connor?" Had she been responsible for his death? She stepped back with angst.

"Fear not, Trinity." Connor approached and flashed the gentle smile she remembered and always took solace in.

Connor appeared very much like her father did—young, radiant, and so much at peace. Not at all what she'd expected from her very last memory of him. The brutality of blood and gore, the pain and suffering he had to have endured before he finally died.

"Uncle, I'm so...." She whimpered and broke into tears. "I'm so sorry."

Connor collected her in his strong arms and hushed her. "You had nothing to do with it, sweet Trinity."

She sucked in a shuddering breath. "I didn't do this to you?" She pulled back, swiping her tears away with the back of her hand.

"Is that what you fear?" He brushed her hair back from her face and met her gaze. "Not at all. You would never be capable of violence, not like that." He kissed her forehead. "A street criminal became crazed. He broke into the apartment and knocked you out. He...murdered me, in a blind rage."

"But why?" She clung to him and sobbed. "You were such a good man."

He shushed her. "It wasn't his fault."

"What?" She tugged back and stared at him in disbelief. "He murdered you. How could you say, after the unspeakable things he did to you, it wasn't his fault?" Rage burned deep in her belly at the preposterous notion.

"The mortal did not act of his volition, my darling. Much like another person you are so very angry with." A soft voice spoke from behind Trinity, one she knew all too well.

She swung around and snarled. "Mother?"

There in front of her stood the one person she had no desire to see. Trinity glared at her, resentment festering deep inside as more tears gathered at the rims of her eyes.

"I realize you blame me—"

"You have no right to be here," she hissed.

"Trinity Sybil McWraith." Her father raised his voice. Even in the faint memories of her childhood, he never scolded her. "You are here for a purpose, and that is to learn the truth, so that you may heal."

Reduced to her inner six-year-old complacency, she gawped at her father. "Yes, Daddy."

"Trinity, the man who killed your uncle was under the same influence I was when I...."

Trinity glanced to find her mother's picturesque porcelain features marred by sadness and shame. "Influence?" She knew what she meant but needed to hear it from her mother's lips.

"The Furies tormented the man who murdered Connor, much the same as they did me, and now as they do with you."

"Why? What have you done to bring the curse of

the Furies down upon us, Mother?" She sneered. "I know they were merely contracted to do the dirty work of someone you pissed off."

Chapter Seventeen

The billowy white clouds overhead began to roll faster. They clustered and darkened into a menacing gray. The wind gusted and whipped Trinity's hair about her face.

"What's happening?" She fisted her hands at the sides of her thighs and scanned the ominous sky.

"The Furies approach as we speak," her father cautioned.

"But they said the Furies can't come into the Elysian Fields?" She glanced around for any sign of the Dread Ones.

"They can't, but they are close in your realm. We haven't much time." Her mother gripped her wrist.

"Arawn, Kane?" Trinity's breath caught in her throat.

"Listen," her mother insisted. "You are in grave danger."

Her father stepped beside her mother, and her uncle joined him. All three faced her.

"I'm on a para hit list, as each of you were. I need to know why," she growled with frustration to her mother. "What did you do to bring this onto us?"

"Nothing." Her mother's eyes welled up.

"You had to have done *something*," she insisted.

Her father narrowed his eyes. "No, but your mother had been cursed. Her entire bloodline is."

"Why?"

"Perhaps the explanation would best come from me, since I am the reason the curse was unleashed." Another woman spoke as she approached Trinity's mother's side.

"Who are you?" She glared at the newcomer who bore a remarkable resemblance to Trinity's mother, Lila.

"I am Aileen." The beautiful stranger gave a slight bow. "Your grandmother."

"Grandmother?" She stared in disbelief.

She had never seen photographs of her grandparents. In fact, she had very few of her family. Over the years, she'd chalked it up to the continual moves she and her uncle made and never questioned it. Connor never spoke of them and said little about her parents over the years.

"Your grandfather is sovereign of the banshee," her grandmother continued.

"What?" Trinity snapped.

Her mother released her grip on Trinity's wrist. "My father is a cruel man, a banshee. His bloodline always held one male for every generation. He believed pure breeding would strengthen the dominance of males, but, as you know, the banshee breed is mostly women." She eased back, her eyes filled with sorrow.

Aileen nodded. "We tried for years to have a child, but the difficulty with male banshees is procreation."

"How so?"

"Their genetics are not strong enough to sustain pure bloodline procreation." Her father spoke low and clear. "That is why the women take on mortal mates, to ensure the banshee do not die out."

"Wait." Her head crowded with the overload of information. "Do you mean to tell me that you aren't my father either?"

"No." He shook his head. "I was fortunate enough to produce a child with my wife, but male banshees don't often have such luck."

"So, how did this result in a curse?"

"The longer it took for me to have a child," Aileen continued, "the more vicious he became. He had never been a man of love or virtue. He threatened to kill me and take a new wife. So...."

"So you strayed, with an empath." Trinity began to piece together the whole story.

"Ayden was a kind man, a gentle spirit. He knew we could not see each other again but vowed to keep my secret. He blessed me with a daughter." Aileen put her arm around Lila. "It seemed fine until she grew into her adolescence and her talents emerged."

"Talents?" Trinity thought for a moment. "Her empathic abilities?" She glanced to her mother.

"Yes. We tried to hide them, but the older I got, the more suspicious your grandfather became."

"Your mother and I met," her father interjected. "We fell in love before things got bad."

A crack of lightning lit up the sky, and thunder boomed long and deep, shaking the ground they stood on.

"Your grandfather confronted me," Aileen continued. "I tried to protect my daughter and my lover, but he tortured me, mercilessly until I confessed." She wrapped her arms around herself and sobbed.

"When he found out the truth, what happened?" Fire coursed through her veins as her hidden history was brought into the light. The truth shot pangs of guilt and remorse through her chest at the sight of the torment her family continued to endure.

"The sovereign executed me on the spot and sent a search party out for my daughter."

"I overheard the Tiwaz Warriors," her father went on. "They were ordered to seek and slaughter Lila and her birth father. I managed to get to her before they found her, and we slipped away."

"And her father?"

Aileen shook her head. "It was too late. He had already been put to a brutal death."

"That's when we moved to the mundane world to hide from the sovereign. Connor took us in and helped us raise you."

"How does all this translate into a curse?" Trinity's confusion lingered. How could her own grandfather have done this to his wife? Even if his daughter was not of his blood, how could he condemn her to such a horrific fate after all those years of raising her as his own child? What kind of heartless monster was he?

This bastard robbed her of the family she was born to, the family she deserved. He had no right.

"When he couldn't find Lila, he ordered the Furies to track her down to exact justice, for her mother's sins, and for being a half-breed. He also ordered them to annihilate any offspring she may have had. He didn't know about you at the time, but the Furies continue their mission until it is complete." Tired wouldn't have described anything her grandmother exhibited. She was depleted on every level of her existence, but, as she shared her tale, an odd relief seemed to fill her weary eyes.

"But Uncle Connor is human?"

"Half, but yes. And he loved and protected you all the same. Remember, my darling"—her mother cupped her chin—"the Furies cannot directly harm anyone. They can drive them insane, or force an innocent to do their bidding."

"Why did I cry tears of blood?"

"That was the Furies. Their eyes drip with the blood of vengeance. When they forced you to see the coming deaths of those you loved, it was part of how they drive you mad, to torment you. Banshees do not cry tears of blood," Aileen offered.

The slithering sense of violation that had festered deep inside her morphed into a frenzy of rage. "How can I defeat them?"

"You take away their power to harm you. Right now is part of it. You have learned the truth, so they cannot affect you anymore, at least not with the past. However, they can still manipulate your perceptions of the present and the future. Beware of them."

"There is something else you must know, my daughter." Her father brushed his knuckles along her jaw. "The sovereign has much more power now than he ever had before. He has collaborated with other para rulers. They have created a sacred alliance."

A sacred alliance? "For what?"

"To rise up against the Syndicate." Aileen lifted her chin and narrowed her eyes.

"Why?"

"We do not know," Aileen replied. "But many will perish and suffer horrible fates if they are not stopped."

A bolt of lightning struck a nearby oak tree and sent it crashing to the ground.

"The Furies are here, in your realm. They search for you now," Aileen cautioned.

"My mates?" Trinity clasped her hand on her cheek. "I have to go." She glanced to her family as tears stung her eyes. "I'm sorry you have all suffered so, but I'm thankful to find you at peace."

She threw her arms around her father's neck and

squeezed him hard as he hugged her back. Connor was next, and she paused in front of Aileen, the grandmother she'd never had. "I wish I could have known you."

"We will meet again, a long time from now, child." Aileen took her into a warm embrace and then retreated with a gentle smile.

Trinity glanced at her mother, and the remnants of resentment dissolved. "I'm sorry I've been so angry with you. I didn't know."

Lila's tears spilled down her porcelain face. "You couldn't have. Just know this, my darling daughter. I am honored to have had you. You are an exquisite woman, full of kindness. I am so proud of you." Lila took her into her arms and nearly squeezed the breath out of her. "I love you, my sweet daughter."

"I love you, too...Mother."

Chapter Eighteen

The trees thrashed about from the velocity of the wind. Fork lightning streaked across the sky.

"I can't hold the conduit much longer." Arawn crouched on his knees. The gnarled wood of the tree trunk dug through the material of his pants into his flesh. Blasts of wind nearly knocked him over. He held his hands and kept the turnstile open. "Come on, princess," he prayed. His cheeks blazed with fire, and beads of sweat dripped down his face and into his eyes. The sting grew. His arms throbbed from the intensity of the swirling energy.

"Hang on, Arawn," Kane called out over the rush of the air.

"Kane," he bellowed. "Here she comes. Get ready to grab her. It's gonna be a bumpy landing." He panted, the last of his strength draining as the shift in weight inside the conduit shoved against his diaphragm. "Come on, baby." He gritted his teeth, determined to sustain. The water subsided a little around the edges of the whirlpool, and the glint of white hair surfaced. "Grab her!"

Kane reached in, gripped her hand with his, and tugged hard. "I've got her." He gave a final yank, and their banshee flew out of the vortex so fast she toppled Kane over onto the ground. "She's clear!"

Arawn released the force field and collapsed beside the oak tree with exhaustion. All three gasped for breath. Rolling to the side, he found Trinity sprawled on top of Kane, both grinning and winded.

"I finally got tackled by you," the gargoyle groaned with amusement.

A bolt of lightning struck a tree just feet away from them, and Arawn bolted upright, his heartbeat racing. "We have to get you out of here." He scrambled to his knees and held his hand out to help her to stand.

"Wait." She glanced all around. "Where is Cemil?"

"He's looking for Brody." Kane clambered to his feet.

"Brody is doing this?" She frowned at Arawn. "Is he dreaming again?"

"No." He didn't want to tell her, fearful she would insist she stay in the midst of life-threatening danger.

"Tell me," she demanded.

A burst of wind blasted so hard it nearly slammed the three of them over. Thunder rolled long and deep as Trinity and Arawn got to their feet.

"A security team radioed." He held up his small radio unit. "Brody took off from the barracks. He was upset."

"Upset? As in sad?" She narrowed her eyes.

"No," Arawn admitted. "In a blind rage."

The faint rose of her cheeks flushed to gray. "By the gods...."

Arawn gripped her shoulder. "What is it?"

"A blind rage. It's the Furies." Trinity furrowed her brows. "Where did he go?"

"We're not sure. Deeper into the forest." Knowing she would take off, Arawn grabbed her arm. "Rekkus is out there. He'll keep Cemil safe. We have to go."

"No! Don't you see? They're using Brody to get to me. He's an innocent boy, and people will get hurt. I have to put an end to this now."

"What can you do, Trinity? They want you dead." Kane let out a ferocious growl.

"They'll leave him alone if they find me. I won't have anyone else harmed, not because of me." Trinity dashed into the open field and hollered for Brody and Cemil. She disappeared into the trees beyond the lavender.

"Wait!" Arawn started after her, but Kane held him back. "What in Tartarus are you doing? They'll kill her." He tried to jerk free.

"Kane, Arawn, I need you. Do you copy?" Rekkus' voice crackled over the handheld unit.

He snagged it off his belt and pressed the button. "This is Arawn. Trinity is back and headed your way."

"Kane, unit eight spotted the Dread Ones in the air. They're heading here."

"Copy that." Arawn released the button, panic and rage coursed through his veins. "We have to find her, now."

"Listen." Kane let out a deep growl. "If we chase her, we can't protect her. Rekkus needs my help. You follow, but keep your wits about you. It's the only way to keep her safe."

He was right. The mere thought of Trinity in danger drove Arawn half out of his mind. "Okay. Rekkus. What is your location? Kane is on his way, over."

"I'm at the north end of the conduit forest."

"Copy that." He tucked the radio back on his belt and looked to Kane.

"You take the ground. I'll go by air to Rekkus." Kane tore off his T-shirt. "There's no time to lose."

"What? You're okay to let her see you shift?" Arawn choked out.

"If I don't, we lose the vantage point to protect her. If she sees me and never wants me again, that's a risk I'll have to take. We can't let them hurt her."

Kane crouched and let the shift take hold. His face contorted with agony; his tanned flesh morphed into a slate-gray, leathery skin. He let out a torturous roar as his wings sprouted from his shoulder blades and his talons protruded. In moments, he was fully shifted into his gargoyle form and stood nearly eight feet tall. He spanned his wings, flapped hard and fast, and took off into the sky. Arawn followed on the ground.

***

Trinity's legs strained as she bolted through the tall flowers against fierce winds. She halted by a cluster of pine trees when a black fog-like energy field radiated behind the massive trunk of a Dragon's Blood tree.

"Brody, listen to me." Cemil's voice was strained.

Trinity scanned the nearby brush, to find Cemil sheltered on the other side of the gnarled and twisted wood. "They're messing with your mind." Cemil's aura glowed with red fear.

Trinity snuck up behind him. "Let me talk to him. Please, get out of here."

"I can't leave you two here alone." Cemil pointed to two armed security guards twenty yards or so behind Brody. They tucked down and hid but aimed what looked to be dart guns at the teen.

"Give me a chance. I think I can get through to him," she pleaded.

He held his palm up toward the armed men,

motioning them to wait. "But don't go out into the open until he's calm," he cautioned her.

Trinity patted his hand. She surveyed the black aura completely enveloping the adolescent. He stood maybe a few inches shorter than her, a gangly lad with wild, blond curls and bright amber eyes widened with terror. He shrieked and howled with delirium.

"Brody, my name is Trinity. I'm a friend of Cemil's."

"I don't have any friends," he wailed in a squeaky, unsteady voice. "Leave me alone. You're the reason. It's all your fault," he hissed at her.

Three fierce flashes of fork lightning blazed across the ominous sky. Thunder boomed and vibrated all around and under their feet. Wind gusted about them, forming mini dust funnels that whipped the lavender stems back and forth. The force of flying debris of sand and leaves stung her cheeks.

"Brody...." Trinity delved into his thoughts—a muddle of burning red, ill-omened black, and sheer hatred. She closed her eyes and focused on how his heart punched against his chest, his pulse thrummed behind his ears with a deafening intensity. Nausea overwhelmed him and bile rose in his throat. Fear and devastation overrode even the most basic of his emotions. This boy had become riddled with the frenzy of rage, a volume so colossal, she wouldn't have read this much on the entire island filled with paras and humans alike, even if they were engaged in a full-fledged war. The psychic assaults on Trinity by the Dread Ones paled in comparison to the torment they perpetrated onto this poor child.

"Tell me what you want." She sensed the emotional pillar the Furies played on, the teen stuck on how he never felt loved or cared about. Beneath the layers of resentment and hostility, there lay a deep-seated sorrow and...guilt? Emotions she was all too familiar with. "Who did you lose, Brody?"

"Get out of my mind," he screeched and, gripping his palms over his ears, he dropped to his knees.

Trinity moved from behind the tree and slowly approached. Cemil grabbed her arm, and she raised her palm. "I've got this. It's okay. Trust me."

Cemil let go and pursed his lips before he nodded.

Trinity moved toward the boy with her hands open in front of her in a show of support. "I feel your grief, Brody. Your father?"

"Stop it. I can't take the voices anymore." He yowled and curled into a fetal position on the ground.

A crack of lightning struck a tree feet away from them, the top branches bursting into flames.

"Get out of here," Cemil hollered over the commotion of the wind.

Trinity glared at him and motioned with her finger for silence.

"The three women in your head?" She knelt on the ground beside Brody, careful to use a calming voice. "I can see them."

"Yes, they're telling me to do terrible things," he wailed.

"They want you to destroy things and hurt people."

"They want me to strike you with lightning and burn you alive," he whimpered helplessly.

"I know. I also know it's not who you are. You're not a violent person. They hurt me, too, Brody. I can help you make them stop." Reaching out, she rested her open palm on the side of his head. "I know it hurts. It feels like a knife stabbing through your brain." She winced, trying to ward off the secondary pain.

"How? I can't block them out, my father—"

"I can see what they've done. They've made you think you killed your father." She caressed his arm.

"I did! It's all my fault. I got mad at him then I blew up the furnace."

"No, Brody. Open your eyes and look at me, right now," she commanded in a firm, but calm voice.

The teen complied, forcing his eyes open as he panted with fear.

"Brody, listen. They did the same to me. They make us see things that aren't real. That is not how your father died."

Trinity motioned Cemil to come closer. She closed her eyes, searched his thoughts for the information she needed, and she found it. "Brody, your father died in a car accident. Do you remember that?"

Another flare of lightning lit the sky, the crack of thunder pierced her ears, and rain dropped in a sudden torrential downpour. She sensed the shift in his emotions—she was breaching his wall of rage and piercing the veil of sorrow that fueled the Furies' wrath.

"Brody, you know this. Think back, before they came to torment you last night. You've been here all week. You've worked with Cemil to get past your loss. It was an accident. You were in school when it happened. It wasn't your fault. There was no explosion, no furnace. You did nothing wrong."

The downpour lessened, and the wind died down. Thunder rolled in the distance, and Brody released his death grip on his ears. He stared up at Trinity as tears spilled down his face. "That's right. I wasn't there."

"Sit up." She shushed him and sat cross-legged. Trinity collected the teen in her arms and hugged him tight. "You did nothing wrong. I'm so sorry you lost your dad." Tears stung her eyes. Her sorrow crashed to the surface and met his. She really did understand his emotions.

Brody melted in her arms, curling up like a baby as he wept—they both did. For the first time in months, Trinity released her sadness and tears she'd worked so hard to mask. He clung to her neck and unleashed his concealed sorrow. "That's it, sweetie. Good job, Brody. They can't hurt you anymore. They have no power over you." She rocked him back and forth until his sobs lessened. "They have no power over either of us anymore, I promise you."

Chapter Nineteen

The rain stopped, the winds calmed, and Brody settled back into a normal adolescent with swollen red eyes and puffy lips from his emotional release. "I'm so sorry I caused all of this."

"Hey," Trinity prompted him with a finger under his chin to meet her gaze. "No more guilt, for either of us, remember?"

"I promise." Brody threw his arms around her neck and held on for a long hug.

"After I take care of a few things, we'll spend some more time together before we have to go home, okay?"

"Deal." The gangly lad's freckled face lit up with the first smile she had seen from him.

"All clear here, sir," one of the armed men spoke into the radio unit.

"Be advised, we are heading to you now. Stay put." Rekkus' voice crackled.

"Copy that," the bald para replied.

"And stay out of sight," Rekkus ordered.

"Yes, sir."

"This isn't over yet. He shouldn't be here any longer, in case they try something else." Trinity offered caution to Cemil. An inner strength she had lost sight of for a long while resurfaced, along with her confidence.

"You're right. I'm gonna get Brother Nature back to the barracks." Cemil grinned and tucked his arm over the boy's shoulder. "Rekkus and the guys will be here in a minute." He nodded to the armed men in cargo pants and jackets. "These two guards will stay with you until they arrive."

"Take care." She winked at Brody and waved good-bye.

Cemil and the lad headed out to the open field. A glimmer on the ground caught her eye. She bent to examine and discovered a silver necklace had fallen on the ground. She opened the rectangular locket and found two small photos, one of a baby and the other of a man who looked very much like her new young friend. "Oh, this must be Brody's," she gasped. "I'll be right back."

Trinity bolted out into the field. "Brody, you dropped this."

Cemil and the teen turned toward her. Their weary, yet light-hearted expressions morphed into ones of horror.

"Trinity, look out!" Cemil pointed to the air.

"Get down," the men behind her yelled.

Before she could spin around to see what the commotion was about, flaps of wind rushed over her and sharp stings pierced both of her upper arms. A brute force lifted her up from the ground. The security guards gripped her ankles and tried to tug her free, but they dangled in the air and slipped, landing on the ground with thuds.

Trinity screamed and, twisting her head upward, she shrieked at the hideous creature carrying her high up into the clouds. Two more flew on either side of them. *The Furies!*

They carried her toward the forest.

"Put me down," she screeched with rage.

"Soon enough, we will leave you to your accord, but for now, we take you away from those who interfere with our duty," the one on her left with dangling red serpents for hair hissed.

They carried her through the deep forest and set her down on a branch on top of one of the tallest oak trees. Standing on the thick limb, she clutched the trunk tight, terror ripping through her chest.

"You can't kill me," she scowled. "I know all about you."

"So you may think, half-breed." One landed on the edge of the branch, causing it to waver. She spanned her decrepit wings to steady herself.

The other two landed on nearby limbs as they took turns taunting Trinity. Each of the former beauty queens were now horrid winged women, all draped in tattered black cloth, their repulsive jagged teeth dripping with ooze. Their previous features and figures, which would have made movie stars swoon, had been replaced with hair of hideous hissing serpents, one yellow, one red, and one black. Their black eyes all dripped with blood. Their wings of pale gray were reminiscent of rotting skin. A wretched odor emanated from them, reeking of death and decay.

"We do not kill. We simply give you a reason to take your own life." The one in front of her crowed.

Instead of petrified, as Trinity had expected to be, she was desperate to piece the last several weeks together to make sense of it all. "Did you steal my clothes at the hot springs?"

"Yes," Red hissed.

"And my bathing suit?"

"We did, along with everything else you couldn't

find," her tormentor snarled. "Including your precious talisman."

"For what reason?"

"What better way to drive someone mad than to make them believe they have misplaced everything?" Yellow Snakes cackled. Her malicious giggle crept down Trinity's spine.

"And to steal their memories, don't forget, dear sister," the hag with black serpent hair declared.

"Why are you doing this?"

"We follow our masters' orders. You shall die by your own hand," the yellow one bit out.

"I know all about my grandmother Aileen, and my grandfather is crazy. This ends now."

"A banshee who bedded the mortal empath; 'twas unfitting of a Bean Nighe."

"So you go around and punish the innocent because a jealous psychopath said so?" Trinity spewed with hatred.

"We serve the justice, but it is the curse handed down by a begrudged husband. You are the last of your mixed line. Once you are dead, no other shall live, and the curse will be done," the one in front of her snarled.

"I know everything now. You have no more power over me. You can't drive me mad anymore."

"Oh, but we will, my pretty," the yellow one taunted. "We have plans for your brooding para hunks, too."

Desperation mounted. *Not them, too. Not because of me.* A bleak possibility clouded her weary brain. "If I don't fight you, if I let you punish me for the sins of my grandmother, will you leave Arawn and Kane alone?"

"That, we cannot." The black snaked one scowled.

"Why?"

"More justice. It is no concern of yours."

"The hell it isn't," she roared. "Tell me now. How can I end this?"

The red serpent-haired sadist waved her triangular ring toward Trinity and let out a venomous hiss. "Die."

A flood of crimson washed over Trinity's vision. Fire burned through her head and her chest. Flashes of her immortal and her gargoyle saturated her brain with stabbing pain. Images of a bloody massacre, skin peeled from their bodies sliced open from neck to sternum, the hounds of hell with red ears, feasting on their flesh.

Driven by instinct, she crouched on the branch and outreached her shaking hands. From deep in her solar plexus, she let out a horrific wail. She screamed so hard and so loud, her eardrums nearly shattered. Heated wetness trickled from her eyes and streamed down her face. Her locked muscles loosened as she expelled the last of her cry. Trinity panted for breath and hugged the trunk of the tree. Her throat stung from the wail.

No," she screamed. "Not them, by the gods, not them." She wept hysterically.

"Trinity?" a deep voice roared.

"It's him again," the red one sneered.

"No mind, the deed is done. She has foreseen the death of both her mates. Leave her to him." They took off, flying into the air, leaving Trinity grief-stricken.

Her mind spun. Her vision faded, and she lost her balance, toppling over and dropping out of the tree. Her stomach bottomed out as she plummeted, but a sudden grip around her waist halted her in midair.

"Trinity," the deep husky voice called to her.

She glanced up to find a gray-winged mass encased her. "Kane," she whimpered.

"Your eyes," he growled. "Hang on." He swooped down with his massive wings and carried her to the field. Her vision cleared as the red faded away. Her chest tightened when Arawn ran over and scooped her up into his arms. She glanced back to find a huge gargoyle staring at her, his eyes filled with sadness.

"Rekkus needs you for air support to make his plan work. You're the only wings we have right now, Kane. She's been hurt, badly." Arawn's voice was strained.

"Stay here in the open." Kane hovered as he looked her over.

Arawn radioed in. "Rekkus, we've got Trinity, over."

"Copy that," his voice crackled. "Kane, be advised, we have it ready, over."

"He's on his way." Arawn clutched the radio and wrapped his arm around her.

"I'm close by. I have you in my sights, I swear it." Kane stared at Trinity then darted back into the air and flew away.

"Are you okay?" Arawn cradled her in his arms and whispered into her ear.

"Stay away," she sobbed hysterically. "You're going to die because of me."

"Princess, your eyes, you're bleeding." He traced her cheek then showed her the bloodied pad of his finger. "Are you hurt?"

Trinity's head stabbed with pain, her chest constricted, and she wheezed for air. Then, his words sank in. "My eyes? Tears of blood?" A sudden angry calm washed over her, and she sat up. She swiped her finger across the wetness lining her eyes and trailing down her face. She examined the crimson, a flash of her parents and grandmother piercing the foggy veil of panic encasing her mind. "Banshees don't cry tears of blood, but the Furies' eyes drip with the blood of vengeance," she recited.

"Yes, you gave the banshee wail.... Are our deaths what you saw?"

"Those evil bitches." She clambered to her feet and bellowed, "It's not going to work, you hear me, you sadistic hags?"

"Whoa, stay with me," he pleaded and tugged at her hand.

"I know your trickery, I'm done with you, come out and face me, you wretched cowards." She thrashed her fist in the air.

"Arawn," Rekkus called over the radio. "I need you both to head back into the forest, over."

Trinity spotted three dark shadows dart across the sky, way up in the gloomy clouds.

"Copy that," he hollered into the walkie-talkie. He grabbed Trinity's hand. "Can you run?"

"I think so." Her upper arms stung. She glanced down to find several puncture wounds across both her biceps. Her knees were weak, but adrenaline coursed through her veins. "I'm fine."

"Come with me. Let's end this now." He bolted toward the trees.

Trinity's legs strained to keep pace with him. Mere seconds into the clearing, the shadows overhead darkened. The Furies made a frantic descent toward them. Their claws extended, they dove down fast.

"Arawn, I've got her," Kane cried out from up ahead. Just before the winged hags reached her, he swooped down and clutched her in his grasp. "I've got ya, darlin'," he called out in a voice much deeper than usual.

Trinity glanced back to find Arawn face down on the ground, the Furies in hot pursuit of her and her gargoyle. He flew fast and furious toward the treetops.

"Kane?" She gripped his arms with fright.

"Don't worry. This is gonna work." He wrapped his leathery wings around her and spiraled toward a small gap between treetops. "Now," he roared.

A clatter of branches cracking and leaves rustling sounded behind them, but from inside his protective wings, she saw nothing. Hideous screeches cried out. Kane opened his wings and landed on a thick limb of a tree. He set her down.

"It's over," he rumbled and nodded down toward the ground.

Trinity glanced down to the sea of lavender, a massive heap of netting entangled over the hags.

"Got 'em." Kane scooped her up and headed down to Arawn.

Chapter Twenty

S itting on a bale of hay inside the entrance of the kennels, Trinity cringed at the sting of topical treatment Arawn applied to her open wounds. "Ouch!"

He winced. "Sorry. Almost done, babe." He bandaged her arms with skill and precision. "Good as new. Now, Sage told me to make sure I give you this." He held up a small brown bottle and removed the squeeze top to reveal a dropper filled with dark-gold liquid.

"What's that?"

"Oil of oregano. The puncture wounds could be contaminated. Who knows what infestation those hags are filled with? It goes under your tongue." He aimed into her open mouth and released three drops. "She called it nature's antibiotics."

A sharp sting spread through her tongue, and spice tingled over the sensitive skin of her mouth as the pungent flavor overtook her senses. "Oh, gross." She shuddered.

"That's my girl. It's no ouzo, but it will help fight infection." He twisted the cap back on and placed it along with the bandages back into the first aid kit.

"So, explain to me what in Tartarus just

happened." She willed away the residual nip of the oil.

"Rekkus and Kane set a trap for the Furies."

"I missed most of it." Confusion rolled over her fatigued brain.

"He had Sarka and her coven weave netting made from hemp. They anointed it with rosemary and dragon's blood oils, a magical assist, if you will. Kane flew up to help set the nets in the trees."

"How did Rekkus know they would be there?"

"Myron saw it in the cards." He grinned.

"Of course she did," she snickered.

Kane skulked into the entrance of the kennel, stood by the door, and avoided eye contact with her. "Are you okay?" His voice was low.

Trinity studied him. Now in his human form, his aura held a faded gray of worry and fret. She joined him. She permeated his thoughts which she found, sadly, filled with shame.

"Kane," she murmured. "I do see you differently since I've witnessed your shift."

"I know. It was a chance I had to take. I couldn't let them hurt you." He turned to leave.

"Wait," she demanded and pulled at his shoulder. "Face me."

Kane complied but cast his gaze to the ground.

Trinity cupped his handsome face between her hands and prompted him to make eye contact with her. His brilliant emerald orbs had dulled with sorrow. "I see you as even more beautiful than before."

He arched his brows. "What?"

"I'm a banshee, you're a gargoyle, and he's an immortal. We are one hell of a team." She stood on her tippy-toes and stole a tender kiss from him. "You don't frighten me."

"I don't?" His worry lightened, and the corners of his full lips curled upward.

"Not at all, Kane. You excite me. You keep me safe, and you make me feel...alive."

Her gargoyle wrapped his arms around her waist and hugged her tight. "Thank the gods. You're incredible," he whispered into her ear.

Trinity pulled back to find his eyes glistening. She rested her hand on his chest and cherished the thumping of his heart against her palm. "Arawn?" She called him over, and he joined them.

Flashing a mischievous grin, Trinity faced her handsome men. "If you'll have me, I consider you both my mates."

Arawn glanced at Kane and winked. "We wouldn't have it any other way." He planted a feathery kiss on her lips.

"Looks like you're stuck with us, darlin'," Kane concurred then stole his sweet kiss.

"But before we get to the good stuff"—Arawn nodded toward the entrance where Rekkus and Cyrus entered—"we have some loose ends to tie up."

The men approached. "Arrangements have been made," Cyrus noted. "The Furies are contained in iron cuffs and chains, in a cell in the kennel here until they can be safely transported through the portal to Kaleb."

"Kaleb?" Trinity glanced to Arawn.

"Para Elite Forces. He's the boss who sent us here for training this week, and Serena's husband."

"Remind me to thank him later." She bit her lips to conceal her giddy grin.

"Arawn, you lead the interrogation since you know more about them personally. We'll listen, and you'll need this." Cyrus handed him a crudely fashioned square.

"What's that for?" Trinity studied the unimpressive box.

"Iron can confine any enchanted tools. They need to be disarmed." Arawn tucked the box under his arm. He motioned to the kennels. "Shall we?"

Trinity stuck close to Arawn's side, hesitant to say anything. The cell of cinderblock walls was enclosed with an iron gate, the cement floor strewn with straw. The three repulsive hags sat side by side, chained to chairs as they awaited confrontation. Their chains were anchored to the walls. Tiny rays of sunlight beamed through a miniscule window at the top with more iron bars which allowed air and light in but no promise of escape. A bleak, dank encasement for her now helpless tormentors, which still didn't fit her idea of the persecution they very much deserved. Not just because of what they did to her and her family, but how they'd used and tormented young Brody to do their bidding. The word evil didn't do them justice.

Arawn started out with a stern glare. "Who sent you?"

"You'll find out soon enough," the yellow-snaked one retorted.

"Let's face it, Arawn." Kane donned a cocky smirk and circled the hideous creatures of olive-gray flesh. "They don't know anything. They're hired hands, with no minds of their own."

"We know everything we need to know, stone creature," one snapped. The red serpents in her hair hissed and slithered around her hideous head.

"Traitor!" the black serpent-haired one barked. "Retribution will crash down upon you."

"Traitor?" He chuckled. "You think you know me?"

"We know each and every one of you. You shall all perish at the hands of the Rescission." Red glared and bared her jagged green teeth.

"The Rescission?" Arawn pursed his lips. "So that's the name they go by?"

"Shut up, Tisphone!" the black one sneered.

"I am sick to death of your nagging, Alecto!" she barked back and struggled to break free.

"Alecto. Then that means the yellow-snaked freak here is Megaera?" Kane smirked. He had successfully manipulated their resolve to stay silent. He took his place at Trinity's side.

"Now we have our introductions finished, let's get down to the nitty-gritty." Arawn stepped closer. He honed his attention on the red one. "Why did they send you after Trinity?"

"Burn in Tartarus," she hissed.

"That much, I can tell you," Trinity spoke up. "My grandfather is the sovereign of the banshee."

"You are of no blood to the sovereign," Tisphone, the red one snarled.

"No, I'm not, I'm thankful to say, because the sovereign was infertile." The truth she learned of her family history offered Trinity a sense of strength. She knew this entire nightmare had been manufactured by a flawed being who didn't measure up as a man in his own eyes. "When my grandmother couldn't conceive his child, he threatened to kill her, so she strayed with an empath, and my mother, Lila, was born."

"An impure spawn who had to be destroyed." Slime oozed down Tisphone's grotesque teeth as she spat her hateful words.

"They managed to hide my mother's true paternity until her empathic talents emerged in her teens. My father saved her life and hid her away in the mundane world, while the sovereign murdered both my grandparents and cast a curse on my bloodline."

"They will obliterate the weakness of the paras who crossbreed," Tisphone yammered.

"I don't buy it." Kane shook his head and pressed his lips tight. "Weakness from crossbreeding?"

Arawn propped one hand on his hip and narrowed his eyes. "Prior to abdicating my claim to the throne, I had an eternity to observe the inner workings of the Underworld leadership. The Patriarchs don't fear weakness. They covet it."

"You know nothing of the matter," Tisphone sneered.

"What they fear," he continued with tenacity, "is the threat that crossbreeding creates to their rule of the Underworld." He dropped his hand to his side. "When new talents emerge from a blending of species, the new generation becomes unpredictable, which translates to the leaders' inability to control and dominate the masses." He took a fleeting glance back at Rekkus and Cyrus.

"They don't want me dead because I'm weak, but rather because I'm a force to reckon with, as you've all recently discovered." Trinity glared at the hags. "You're now powerless against me. My mother's ability to read the sovereign's evil intentions made her a threat to his rule, not to mention, made him realize his defect of sterility. So, out of this scenario, who is the real weak para, those of us with exceptional gifts and resiliency, or the one with an inability to breed?"

"This is not over. They will come for you...all of you." Tisphone frothed at the mouth as she fumed. "Hate us all you want. We are the enforcers of the Underworld's wrath."

"I don't hate you hags, I pity you." She approached them and curled her lip.

"Pity?" Tisphone snarled. "Why would you pity us?

We drove you and your mother mad," she boasted.

"Because, you wretched hag, with all the power you possess, you're still mindless drones with no free will of your own, whatsoever. You don't have the ability to make choices for yourselves, be it good or bad, but you are governed by loyalty to whoever rules you." Trinity clamped her hand on Tisphone's right wrist and tugged off her chained bracelet then her Rescission ring. She did the same to the other two and dropped the gruesome jewelry into the crudely crafted iron box Arawn held open. "And now, you have no power, over anyone."

A blare of new thoughts screamed inside Trinity's head, and she backed away.

"Torture is it, then?" Alecto snarled. "Or execution? Whatever our fates shall hold, be done with it now."

"We don't torture, unlike you, and we aren't mercenaries." Arawn closed the lid and tucked the sealed iron box under his arm. "You'll be handed to the Syndicate to answer for your crimes against innocent paras. Your fates will be in their hands, not ours." Arawn wrapped his arm around Trinity's shoulders and escorted her out of the cell.

By the entrance of the kennel, Trinity paused and gripped Arawn's hand with fright.

"What is it?" He tilted his head.

"When I took their jewelry off, I read their thoughts for the first time."

"What did you read?" Kane frowned.

"This retribution...it runs way deeper than we thought. I saw a group of different Underworld leaders with several agendas. The hit list runs further than anyone knows. There are several lists, more than even the Furies are familiar with, I'm sure. I saw lists and private meetings with other leaders they weren't allowed into. Each leader who is part of the Rescission has their own, for their self-serving reasons, and their pawns to exact their version of justice."

Kane let out a low growl and stepped closer to Trinity. "How do we find out more about this?"

Cyrus drew in a slow inhale. "We need to hand all the information we have over to the Syndicate."

"Many of them are on the lists, too." Trinity hugged herself to ward off the chills of despair. "But I did sense that there is vulnerability within the Rescission. They're not completely established yet. Because it is disjointed and somewhat anarchic, there is room for the Syndicate to eradicate the uprising before it hits epic proportions."

"For now, we've done all we can here. We'll see what the Syndicate decides is the best course of action." Cyrus nodded.

Rekkus narrowed his eyes and growled at the mention of the Syndicate.

"Can I ask you something, Rekkus?" Trinity raised her brows with curiosity.

"Sure?"

"How did you come up with the idea to trap them with a net?"

He cracked a one-sided smirk. "We've had a few issues with rogue vampire bats who have tried to hunt on the island. It had originally been intended to round them up."

Trinity chuckled and then took note of his stern glare. "Oh, you're serious?"

"Rekkus isn't much for kidding," Arawn whispered beside her ear.

Chapter Twenty-One

"How did we manage to get so lucky?" Kane crooned as he and his comrade plopped down onto the couch in the cabin. "This week, we were supposed to be getting our asses kicked by Rekkus. Instead, we're happily mated with the most gorgeous, intelligent creature we've ever set eyes on." He propped his feet up on the coffee table.

"I'm not sure." Arawn tucked his folded hands behind his head and exhaled. "But I'm grateful."

The handle to the front door turned, and Kane's heart skipped a beat. "She's back." He took his feet down and sat up, eager to greet Trinity.

In she strolled, sporting an ear-to-ear grin. She spun around and waved good-bye before she entered the cabin and closed the door.

"Hello gentlemen." She giggled and sauntered over to them. She twirled around but remained standing, obviously waiting for them to make room for her to sit between them. Kane scooted over and she nestled between them with an exasperated exhale.

"Everything okay, darlin'?" He stroked his fingers through her silky platinum locks. He cherished the softness of her luscious curls and his good fortune of earning her trust and acceptance of him—a gargoyle.

"Couldn't be better." She hummed a cheerful tune.

Kane waited and tapped his foot with impatience. "Well? What did the Rowans want to discuss with you?"

She remained silent while her lips twitched in a mischievous grin.

He glanced at his friend and cocked his head. "I can't be the only one here dying of curiosity, can I?"

"No." Arawn twisted toward her. "Come on, tell us."

"After they saw how I worked with Brody, in dire circumstances, and given my practice in New York has dwindled to nothing, they offered me a chance to remain on the island and offer my services for grief counseling and intuitive healing for guests."

"Really?" Kane's chest tightened with anticipation. "You're gonna stay here, on the island?"

"I am!" She folded her hands and clutched them between her jean-clad knees. "They offered me this cabin, and...."

Kane growled with impatience. "And?"

"It's big enough for three." Her exhilarated demeanor shifted, the corners of her lips curled down, and she lowered her shoulders.

"What's wrong?" Arawn brushed his knuckles along her cheek.

"I could get awful lonely here, all by myself." She hunched her shoulders and stared up at the ceiling.

"Trinity?" Kane smirked. "Any chance you need a couple of roommates?"

"Well...." She shrugged. "If you know anyone who might be interested. I mean, I'm not easy to live with. People have complained about loud screams, the occasional crying, and the fact that I'm a relentless sex addict." She jumped up and waltzed to the kitchen.

"I don't know." Arawn tossed his hands up in the air. "It's a tough sell."

"Get back here," Kane commanded.

Trinity sauntered back to the couch and stood in front of him, hands on hips. "What?"

With a chuckle, he grabbed her wrist and tugged her onto his lap. Arawn inched closer and slipped her legs over the top of his thighs. "You don't have to convince us. We're your mates, remember?"

"How could I forget?" She gazed into his eyes with affection.

Kane devoured her lips with insatiable hunger. Before he got too lost in the moment, he retreated. Concern clouded his joy.

She stroked her fingers through his hair as she stared at him. "What is it?"

"To be clear, being on the Para Elite Force, we travel a lot for work."

"I know all about it. Those were some of the pros and cons we discussed before I accepted."

"You're okay with us being away for sometimes weeks at a time?" Arawn confirmed.

"If there's one thing I've learned, my beloveds"—she glanced back and forth between him and Arawn—"it's that life is short. I'll take whatever stolen moments I can have with you, both of you. If Kaleb and Serena can make it work, I don't see why we can't."

"You're sure we're the right guys for you?" Kane teased.

"Well, the mundane are not strong enough to contend with the likes of me, and I've never grown so fond of any other paras before you two," she crooned.

Kane's heart sank. "You've seen other paras

before?" He cringed as the words slipped out. "Never mind, it's not my business."

"It's okay. Truth is, I dated a were-cat once, but it didn't work out." She flashed a playful pout.

"Why not?" Arawn took the bait.

"It turns out, I'm allergic to cats." She giggled and slapped her thigh with amusement, and they had a good chuckle along with her.

"We need to celebrate, baby." Kane planted a long, slow-building kiss on her lips before he prompted her to her feet.

"How so?"

Arawn stood and adjusted the front of his pants, grimacing.

"Dude," Kane grumbled.

"Unavoidable. She gets me riled up." He tugged the sides of his T-shirt out from his waistband and pulled it over his protruding zipper. "We still have Twister and some ouzo." He snickered.

"As I recall, we owe you a massage," Kane declared with triumph.

"Pampering with the hands of my beloveds. I can handle it." Their banshee lifted her shirt over her head and dropped it to the floor. Next, she reached behind her and unlatched her pink lace bra and tossed the garment at him. She shuffled toward the king-sized bed and unfastened her jeans as she kicked off her sneakers.

Kane scampered toward the kitchen and fished through the cupboard. He returned to the bed with a jar in hand and held it for Arawn to see. *Coconut oil. Should make for a sensual massage.*

Kane opened the jar and both scooped up a generous amount, the divine aroma wafting up his nose. They knelt on the bed on either side of their naked, waiting beauty. *Damn, she's gorgeous.*

Enamored with her clean-shaven pussy, he licked his lips with anticipation. "Roll over."

Trinity complied and lay on her tummy. He took in the coveted view of her heart-shaped ass. They slathered the slippery oil over her heated skin. Arawn worked her shoulders, neck, and arms. Kane focused on her legs, ass, and lower back. A delicate purr rumbled in her chest and made his cock strain against his zipper.

"I really enjoy this pampering, but there's something I really need right now to soothe my tattered nerves," she moaned.

"Another cup of Sage's herbal tea?" Kane taunted.

She turned her head to the side. "Not what I had in mind, stud muffin." She reached for the button of his pants. "I want your cocks," she crooned and flashed a seductive leer. "Both of them."

Kane glanced at Arawn, and they jumped up and tore off their clothes. Their banshee rolled onto her back and lay waiting. Arawn took point between her thighs while Kane claimed her lips. He swept his tongue into her mouth. She reached for him and teased his length with her fingertips. Kane shuddered under her touch. His flesh came to full attention in her grasp, and she guided him toward her luscious lips. Inch by inch, she took him into her hot, wet mouth. He caressed her tits and brushed over her pink nipples. The peaks stiffened as he pinched and rolled them between his fingers. She cradled his head on her tongue and hummed. The incredible sounds in the back of her throat shot straight to his cock. Eager to drag this session out, he retreated and planted a feathery kiss on her lips again.

"Oh, my." She shivered and glanced down to where Arawn feasted on her. "I need you both inside me."

Their mate gripped Arawn by the hair and pulled him to her kiss. "Please?" she whispered.

Trinity patted the bed for Kane to lie down. Once he'd settled in place, she eased her leg over and straddled him. He gripped his throbbing head and rubbed it along her slick folds. She glanced over her shoulder, where Arawn knelt in place behind her and kissed him hard. She held her hand over Kane's and slipped the tip of his cock into her tight, wet entrance then eased down over his thickness and groaned.

Kane cradled her cheeks with his palms and drew her in for a powerful kiss as she consumed his cock with her pussy. Behind her, Arawn kissed her back and shoulders, and she gasped.

"Are you okay?" Arawn panted.

"Yes, more." She lowered herself all the way down to the base of Kane's cock and held tight as Arawn pushed into her ass. She whimpered with elation. "Yes!"

They moved together in sensual sync. She rode Kane's cock while Arawn pumped into her from behind. Kane massaged her swollen clit and caressed her hip. Their breaths grew punctuated and rhythmic. Their pace quickened, and Kane cupped her voluptuous tits as they bounced up and down from the force. Trinity tilted her head back and groaned with exquisite pleasure. The walls of her pussy contracted around his shaft. She slammed harder onto him and panted.

"Uh, I'm...I'm...." She clamped down hard onto his cock as her muscles constricted around him.

Kane's balls pulled up tight against his body; white-hot tingles spiked through his spine and wrapped around his hips. A quiver danced along his limbs and straight down to the tip of his cock. He held back as long as he could, until the tension broke deep inside him. He roared with completion and pressed hard up into her as he pulsed deep inside.

Arawn groaned long and deep and convulsed against her back. She tremored between them as she slowed her movement over his pulsating cock.

Kane wrapped his arms around her, Arawn dropped onto the bed beside them. "This will be tough to handle." Arawn chuckled.

Kane kissed her forehead and stroked his fingers through her silky locks as he relished their good fortune.

She shuddered and collapsed onto his chest with winded breath. "I'm sure I can get used to this."

Trinity lay on Kane's chest, cherishing the moment as long as she could. The pounding of his heart against her cheek and the stroke of Arawn's hand along the length of her back sent tingles of excitement curling around her spine. She turned her head to glance at Arawn lying beside them and inched down and snuggled up between her gargoyle and immortal.

How fortunate she had become in the face of adversity. Her muscles loosened as she caught her breath, but her mind raced with all she had been through in such a short while. She had been brought to the brink of insanity, lost everyone she had ever loved, and was tormented by evil creatures for a family vendetta she had nothing to do with. She had even lost her career because of this catastrophe.

Now, she found herself mated to the two most, handsome, protective, and devoted men she had ever set eyes on and would live on this incredible island with a brand new career helping others heal from tragedy, all in less than a week? By the gods, they did work in mysterious ways.

"Yes, I can most definitely get used to this."

Trinity kissed Kane's cheek then twisted to the side and captured Arawn's lips with a gentle kiss. Arawn snagged the sheets and draped them over the threesome. Trinity nestled in, Arawn peppered her shoulder with tender kisses, and Kane caressed her cheek as she drifted off into a peaceful sleep.

About the Author

Born and raised in Toronto, Kali now resides in the exquisite eastern Ontario countryside where she enjoys the serenity of nature. When she isn't busy being the married mother of two, certified trainer or counselor extraordinaire, she shadows worlds of paranormal passion & intrigue.

Kali strives to create emotional, compelling stories and characters you can't help but love, hate and cheer for. Captivated by her love of dragons, gargoyles and everything paranormal, she pens these delightful creatures into epic tales of romance and adventure and often infuses her passions of martial arts, music and ironic twists even she didn't foresee.

A good cup of tea with the crackling fire gets her creative juices flowing in the wee hours of the night, when the house is quiet and she can type away to her heart's desire. Learn more at: www.kaliwillows.com

Other Books by Kali Willows

Designing Passion

Damnation and Desire

Savannah's Ghost Tale

Terminal Lust

Double Dragon Seduction

Dragon Temptation

Tantric Storm

Dragon's Breath

Dragon's Bond

Romancing the Author

A Cougar Among Wolves